Office of Scientific Operations

With the conclusion of the traumatic events in 1933 surrounding the shocking affair involving the city of New York and a beast commonly referred to as “King Kong” the president of the United States, Franklin Roosevelt, established the Office of Scientific Operations (OSO). The purpose of the OSO was to monitor, evaluate the level of risk and assist in any manner the mitigation of danger of any and all scientific operations and anomalies. With the rapid pace of scientific discovery this office was given the highest priority and clearance to investigate any potential threats or consequences to the interests of the United States of America.

Office of Scientific Operations - Declassified Files (Release #5)

K McConnell

Published by K McConnell, 2022.

OFFICE OF SCIENTIFIC OPERATIONS - DECLASSIFIED FILES (RELEASE #5)

First edition. June 7, 2022.

ISBN: 979-8230351580

Written by K McConnell.

From the case files of the
Office of Scientific Operations:

Declassified File

Public Release #5A

File #166

1955

Commonly referred to by the public as "Tarantula"

1

They stood in the middle of the street watching the towering flames engulf the monster.

Dr. Matt Hastings stood with an arm around Stephanie "Steve" Clayton, the research assistant for the later Professor Gerald Deemer. Sheriff Andrews was there along with Joe Burch the local newspaper publisher. There were several county and state police present as well and an assorted gathering of the townspeople of Desert Rock, Arizona.

They all were mesmerized by the sight. The silhouette of the giant tarantula was still visible as the massive flames from the napalm the Air Force jets that continued to streak past overhead had just dropped.

"Thank God that's over with." Steve said quietly.

Hastings rubbed her shoulder. "Absolutely."

They watched the scene for another few minutes and then slowly turned and started walking back towards the Palace Hotel.

"What are you going to do now?" Hastings asked. It was obvious that he was subtly asking her to stay in Desert Rock, but he knew she was a scientist and a place like Desert Rock, being a small town out in the desert was not likely to hold much scientific research work for her.

Steve shrugged. She glanced up at Hastings. "I don't know. Professor Deemer's growth serum had so much potential for the future of mankind that I have a hard time just walking away from it."

Hastings nodded. "I understand, but what can you do? What can anyone do? Deemer's research was lost, wasn't it? I mean the tarantula destroyed his entire home, including his laboratory."

"I guess. I mean, the house was crushed, but some of his work might still be buried out there." Steve said.

Hastings shook his head slowly. "I don't know. That place was nothing but rubble when we left it."

"Still. If there's a chance of recovering his work...oh Matt, we've got to try and see if we can find his notes and journals." Steve looked longingly at Hastings.

Hastings met Steve's eyes. He patted her arm. "OK. We can have a look and see."

Steve gave Hastings a quick hug. "Oh, thank you."

Hastings smiled at Steve. "We'll go out there first thing tomorrow." They walked on and into the Palace Hotel and out of the hot sun.

Back in the street Lieutenant Nolan of the Arizona State Police leaned on his car and patted Sheriff Andrews on the shoulder.

"Well, at least that's over with." Nolan said.

The sheriff nodded, his eyes still fixed on the burning carcass of the giant tarantula. "I'll say."

"So, who's going to go out there and clean that mess up?" Joe Burch, the newspaper editor asked with a smile.

Nolan held up a hand. "Sorry. Not the job of the State Police."

Joe looked at Sheriff Andrews who quickly waved it off. "I just keep the peace. I don't clean the streets."

They all laughed—-until the nauseating stench of burning spider hit their nostrils. They quickly retreated back up the street and into the sheriff's office.

The following morning Hastings and Steve drove out towards the wreckage of Dr. Deemer's house. The wind blew their hair about with the roof of the convertible down. It was another cloudless day in the desert and would have been beautiful if in the distance they didn't have to see the scorched remains of the giant tarantula or smell the charred flesh.

They pulled up in front of the collapsed house and parked. Slowly they got out and stared at the pile of rubble that was once both a home and a lab for Dr. Deemer. Steve took a deep breath. She still seemed somewhat shaken by the events just two nights before when the tarantula walked out of the desert and began tearing the house down around Dr. Deemer and her. She watched as Deemer was crushed by the leg of the monster and she was forced to flee the house. If Hastings had not shown up right then she would have been eaten by the creature. They had fled in Hastings' car while the tarantula pursued them.

Steve and Hastings worked their way carefully through the splintered wood and glass of the shattered house. Steve seemed to get braver the further she went into the wrecked house. She seemed increasingly determined.

"Be careful." Hastings said trying to slow Steve down as she pushed further into the mess.

"It's OK." Steve said over her shoulder, but a moment later with groan a wooden beam came smashing down right next to Steve. She jumped with a brief yell.

"This place isn't stable." Hastings said. "I don't think we should be in here."

Steve waved towards Hastings. "It's OK. The lab was just over here." Steve pushed on.

Reluctantly Hastings followed her into another section of the house that once was the lab. There was crushed electronic equipment, smashed cabinets and tables. The cages that held various lab animals were there as well as the dead bodies of the animals. As the temperature of the desert morning increased a smell was rising from the dead animals.

Several times Hastings suggested they resigned themselves to the fact that finding anything useful here was a lost cause. Steve ignored Hastings' words and kept poking around and shoving aside sections of broken wood. Finally, Steve let out a gasp.

"What?" Hastings asked quickly trying to work his way over to where she was.

"It's here." Steve stood up from a pile carefully flipping aside a dead rabbit. She held up a couple of notebooks.

"Are those Deemer's notes?" Hastings asked.

"Yes." Steve said smiling.

"Can we get out of here now?" Hasting asked trying not to stumbled backwards over a squashed filing cabinet.

"Sure Matt." Steve said working her way back out of the lab.

They stepped back out on to the driveway in front of the house and stopped next to the car. Steve couldn't help flipping through several pages of one of the notebooks.

"What exactly are you going to do with those?" Hastings asked. There was a hint of concern in his voice.

"I don't know, but this is too important to be lost." Steve said without looking up from the pages.

"Well, I think it should be turned over to someone, I suppose." Hastings said.

Steve looked up from the notebook at Hastings. "Like who? I probably know as much about this now as anybody."

Hastings nodded cautiously. "That...may be true, but, as we have seen, this stuff can be very dangerous. I think any further work with it should be under a more controlled environment."

"Of course. Of course." Steve said looking back down at the pages of the notebook.

"Seriously, Steve. This whole situation could have turned out far worse than it did." Hastings said.

"I know. I understand." Steve said turning a page.

"Wait. Did you hear something?" Hastings asked. He turned slightly to his left.

Steve glanced up at him. "No. I didn't hear—-" She stopped and lifted her head up a little higher.

They both stood silently for a moment. From somewhere on the other side of the house site there was the sound of rocks rolling. They looked at each other. Slowly Steve set the notebooks down on the hood of the car.

Hastings moved carefully towards the corner of the house, a part of the house that was still partially erect. Steve moved up next to him.

Together they eased around the wreckage of the house. When they reached the back of the house they didn't see anything unusual.

Behind the house was a gentle slope up to a small ridge of rock and sand. Out of the corner of his eye Hastings thought he saw movement at the ridge top. He turned quickly as did Steve, perhaps seeing the same movement. For just an instant it seemed like a patch of something black was there and then it was gone.

"What was that?" Hastings asked quietly.

"I don't know." Steve said. "And I'm not sure I want to find out."

Hastings hesitated. He wasn't sure it was a good idea to go up the ridge and take a look, but somehow he felt like they needed to know if something—-something they didn't want to put into words—-was actually there.

"Stay here." Hastings said and started slowly up the slope.

"Matt, don't. I'm afraid." Steve said.

"It'll be OK." Hastings said and crept up the slope. It took him a couple of minutes to quietly work his way to the top. Once at the ridge Hastings peeked over to the other side. There was a slight breeze and an odd cloud of dust presumably kicked up by the wind, but nothing else. Hastings looked back down at Steve. He shook his head and shrugged down at her. Hastings climbed back down.

"Nothing?" Steve asked.

"Nothing." Hastings said shaking his head. "Maybe we are just a little spooked by the last few days."

Steve nodded. "You're probably right."

They walked back to the car. Hastings turned the car around and starting driving back into town while Steve sat hugging the notebooks.

2

Elliot Simms, government agent of the OSO, the Office of Scientific Operations, sat back in his seat as the plane worked its way over the Rocky Mountains and continued to try to tune out the conversation next to him.

"I don't know. It's...just that there have never been any women in the OSO." Robbie Regan said, also and agent for the OSO.

"Just because there hasn't been any women before doesn't mean there can't be." Beka said pushing back a stray wisp of short blonde hair from her forehead.

"Well, it's...just dangerous work. We get into some pretty tight spots." Regan said.

"Like being in the middle of the Pacific and a giant octopus crushes the boat you're in?" Beka asked eyeing Regan.

"Yeah, well, we did come and save you from being eaten by sharks." Regan pointed out.

Beka smiled. "And that's why the three of us make a good team."

"Not a team." Simms said without opening his eyes.

"We watch out for one another." Beka said.

"Beka there's a lot of training that is required to be in the OSO. And, well, no women have ever been in the OSO." Regan said.

"You already said that. There's a first for everything. Just think of it as on the job training. I'm just a team member in training." Beka said proudly.

"Not a team." Simms said.

Suddenly a stewardess appeared in the aisle next to their seats. She seemed a little anxious.

"Excuse me," The stewardess said, "Is one of you Agent Simms?"

Simms opened his eyes and looked up at the stewardess. "I am."

"The pilot says you have an urgent call coming through. He says you need to come up to the cockpit." The stewardess said.

Simms stood up and followed the stewardess towards the front of the plane.

"Uh, oh. This can't be good." Regan said.

"Well, whatever the mission is, it's nothing we can't handle." Beka said confidently.

"There aren't any women..." Regan's voice trailed off as Beka stared at him.

The stewardess opened the cockpit and ushered Simms in. Both the pilot and the copilot turned and nodded at Simms.

"You're Agent Simms?" The pilot asked loudly while his ears were still covered by his headset.

"I am." Simms replied with a nod.

The pilot gestured to the copilot who pulled his headset off and handed it to Simms.

"Call for you. From Washington. Somebody from...I think it was the OSS." The pilot said.

"OSO." Simms said taking the headset and putting it on.

"What's an OSO?" The copilot called out to the pilot.

The pilot shrugged. "I don't know, but Denver just told us we are diverting to Phoenix so it must something big."

The pilot flicked a couple of switches and pointed at Simms.

"This is Simms." Simms said.

"Elliot." A familiar voice came through the headset.

"Director." Simms replied. It was Marcus the Director of the OSO.

"I need you to check something out." Marcus said.

"OK." Simms said.

"It's in Arizona. A small town by the name of Desert Rock." Marcus told him.

"OK. What's happening there?" Simms asked

"Hopefully nothing. It may be that the situation has already been resolved. The Sands Air Force base just napalmed a giant spider." Marcus explained.

"You said spider?" Simms asked.

"Yes. A spider." Marcus answered.

"Not an ant?" Simms asked.

"No. Not an ant. As far as we know those things are still all dead. This spider seems to have been the result of a lab accident." Marcus said.

"But the spider is already dead?" Simms asked.

"Yes, but I want confirmation of the spider's death, its origins and that there are no more out there." Marcus said.

"Understood." Simms said. He briefly thought about telling Marcus that somehow they were saddled with a civilian that he had been unable to break free of, but thought better of it. Beka was kind of hard to explain. They had saved her from the wreckage of a destroyed boat and she had latched on to them, Regan in particular, because she apparently was a wildly independent woman with no place in particular to go.

"I'll await your report." Marcus said.

"Very good, sir." Simms said and the line clicked off. Simms handed the headset back to the copilot. While he was doing that the pilot was apologizing to the passengers and informing them that the plane was redirecting to Phoenix.

As Simms stepped out of the cockpit the passengers all seemed to be calling out at once. The stewardesses were trying to calm everyone down by assuring them nothing was wrong with the plane. Numerous people at the front of the plane watched Simms emerge from the cockpit and eyed him suspiciously.

Trying to seem innocent and inconspicuous Simms moved slowly down the aisle towards his seat. By the time he reached the row many more eyes were staring at him as if he had just shot everyone's dog. He eased into his seat.

"So, what's the assignment, boss?" Beka asked in a hushed tone.

"Right now?" Simms asked looking at her. "Try not to get strangled by the other 72 passengers before we get to Phoenix."

Beka glanced around at all the eyes staring at them. Slowly all three of them slid slightly lower in their seats. It was going to be a long flight into Phoenix.

3

Hastings reached across the table and took hold of Steve's hand. He smiled at her. The afternoon sun was slowly settling towards a distant ridge.

"So, have you thought about whether you're going to stay here in Desert Rock?" Hastings asked.

Steve shrugged. "I don't know. You know I would like to, but I would need some kind of facility if I want do any further work on Professor Deemer's experiments. That requires financial backing. If I could find that then maybe I could resurrect Professor Deemer's place. If not, well, then I would need to go wherever I could find an existing place to work in."

Hastings nodded slightly. "Right. On the subject of that...are you sure that you can avoid Deemer's mistakes?"

"It wasn't Professor Deemer's fault things got out of control." Steve said defensively.

"I'm not trying to blame anyone. I'm just saying that perhaps with a more secure facility and stronger security all of this could have been avoided." Hastings said.

Steve clearly wanted to say something, but seemed to recognize that there was at least some truth to what Hastings had said.

The door of the restaurant swung open and the few people in the restaurant turned to look. A young man in a cowboy hat and dusty clothes stood just inside the door. He looked around and spotted Hastings. He quickly crossed the room to their table.

"Dr. Hastings, I don't know if you remember me, but..." The young said hurriedly.

"It's Brian, right?" Hastings asked.

Brian nodded. "Yes sir. I work, I mean I worked for Andy, you know, before the monster got him." Brian swallowed.

"Sure. I remember." Hastings said.

"Well, since...since that happened to Andy, I have kind of taken over minding the ranch and well, it happened again." Brian said.

Hastings and Steve stared at Brian.

"What happened?" Hastings asked.

"The cattle. A couple more of them. They're...like the others." Brian spit out.

"Like the others...?" Hastings had an idea what Brian was trying to say, but didn't really want to believe it.

"Dead. Stripped to the bone." Brian said.

"Are you sure they weren't killed a couple of days ago?" Hastings asked.

Brian shook his head. "No sir. I'm sure these were alive last evening."

Steve gasped. "No." She said quietly.

"Damn." Hastings said.

"I tried to find the sheriff, but I couldn't." Brian said.

"The sheriff's gone over to the Pine Bluffs airport to pick up a couple of guys from the government." Hastings said absently.

"What should I do?" Brian asked.

Hastings stood up. "I guess I better have a look. Just to be sure."

Steve stood up as well.

Hastings held up a hand. "You better wait here."

Steve shook her head. "No. I need to know. If there's another one."

"Are you sure?" Hastings asked.

Steve nodded. "I'm sure."

The three of them walked out. Brian climbed into his pickup truck and Hastings and Steve followed him in Hastings' convertible out to the ranch. When they arrived the ranch was bathed in gray light as the hills to the west now cast a long shadow across the place.

Hastings and Steve got out of the car.

"It's around here." Brian pointed towards the back of the large barn.

The three of them walked through a gate into the spacious corral behind the barn. The carcass was immediately visible. It was only about fifteen feet along the fence line from the large barn doors that closed off the inside of the barn from the corral. They walked over to it.

It was just like the dead cattle Hastings had seen here at the ranch days earlier. There was even a small pool of white liquid which Hastings had tested from the other sites and it was determined to be tarantula venom.

"Damn." Hastings said staring down at the remains of the steer. "How could there be another one?"

"Well, it is standard practice to use multiple subjects of the same species when testing the effectiveness of a serum." Steve said.

"So, there were two tarantula test subjects and both of them escaped the lab during the accidental fire." Hastings said.

"Or maybe when the first tarantula destroyed the house." Steve suggested. "Honestly, with all that has gone on, I don't remember which lab animals had been started on the serum which ones hadn't. I would need to go through Professor Deemer's notes to get an inventory of the animals that were actively being tested."

"I think that would probably be a good idea. If there is another tarantula loose out here—-" Hastings was saying.

"If?" Steve glanced over at Hastings.

Hastings waved a hand at her. "OK, since there *is* another tarantula, we should probably determine if it is the only other specimen on the loose."

"OK." Steve agreed.

"We better get back into town and let Sheriff Andrews know what's going on." Hastings said.

They turned away from the dead steer and Brian grabbed Hastings arm.

"What?" Hastings asked.

"Shhh." Brian said.

They stood silent for a moment. Then they heard it. A soft rumbling. It was the sound of rocks and dirt rolling down a hillside.

They turned and looked out past the far end of the corral. There, at the top of the hill beyond the corral the could make out in the dim light the unmistakable shape of a giant tarantula.

Steve let out a short cry. With the sound the tarantula started down the slope of the hill towards them.

"Inside the barn!" Hastings yelled and Brian yanked the barn door open. They scrambled inside and Hastings and Brian quickly slid the door shut. There was no lock to the door, but Brian grabbed some rope lying just inside the door and rapidly tied both sides of the door together so they could not be opened. All three of them backed away from the door.

Minutes passed and nothing happened. All three silently hoped the tarantula had simply passed by the ranch and moved away. The sound of the cattle, which had been hovering around just outside the corral in the hopes of receiving some hay, told them the tarantula was approaching the ranch. The cattle began bellowing and then the sound hooves thumping rapidly away into the field further out indicated the spider was close.

It grew quiet and, again, without a word, all three of them took another couple of steps further back from the door. When the sound did come, it surprised all of them. It didn't come from the door, it came from above them. They looked up to see boards of the curving roof splintering. Pieces of wood began raining down on them.

With a second crash, part of one of the tarantula's legs stuck through the roof. It pulled back tearing more of the roof away. Quickly the three of them backed up towards the front of the barn. Later Hastings would think how stupid he had been for assuming that the tarantula had any idea what a door was and how silly it was that they had been standing there watching the door of the barn.

They were within 15 feet of the front barn door and another round of smashing wood signaled more of the roof was caving in. This time it was along the front of the barn. Large timbers came crashing down right in front of the door, blocking their way forward. They dove backwards to avoid being crushed by some of the falling debris. It was apparent that the tarantula had climbed up onto the roof of the barn and was tearing into it from above.

"Matt!" Steve called out as a long board came down and bounced off of Hastings' shoulder.

Hastings waved at Steve. "I'm OK."

"This way!" Brian yelled as he scrambled through a stall to the side of the barn. Hastings and Steve followed. In the stall there was a narrow gap between two boards. Brian began kicking at more of the planks next to the gap. Hastings joined in as well. After several tries they managed to break enough boards to allow them to squeeze out.

Once out of the barn they ran over to the vehicles nearby and looked back. The tarantula was still on top of the barn, but it was sinking as the weakening roof began to collapse. Moments later the tarantula disappeared into the barn.

"Quick in the car!" Hastings yelled. The three of them piled into the convertible. Hastings started the car and swung it back around. Just as he began pulling away from the barn the front door of the barn burst open. The tarantula shattered more of the front of the barn as it forced its way out through the barn door opening.

Hastings hit the gas and sped down the long driveway of the ranch. After a moment's hesitation the tarantula started running after the car. The car bounced roughly over the sand and gravel drive, but still stayed ahead of the tarantula.

Hastings barely slowed down in making the 90 degree turn out on to the paved road. He stomped on the accelerator and, after a moment of spinning tires, the car took off down the road. The tarantula was still close, but now, on pavement, the car could get sufficient traction to begin leaving the spider behind.

Steve and Brian kept looking back and after Hastings had opened up a half mile distance between them and the tarantula they saw the giant spider stop. It stood, presumably watching them escape. Moments later they could see it moving off in another direction.

4

"Huh. A taxi!" Sheriff Andrews laughed.

"Well, yes, I guess we didn't realize how rural it was out here." Simms said. "We appreciate you driving out here to pick us up."

"No problem. When the State Police told me you guys were coming out here and said they needed to meet you at Pine Bluffs, well, I told them 'No sirree. I'll pick up our boys from the government. It would be my privilege.' Least I can do for Uncle Sam." Andrews said.

"Well, your government thanks you." Regan said.

Andrews eyed Beka. "Didn't know they had women agents now too. Wow, modern times."

"She's not an agent." Simms said.

"I am in training right now, but should be a full fledged agent soon." Beka said.

"Not an agent." Simms said.

Andrews looked confused.

"As we said, it was nice of you to come all the way out here to get us. We...don't always get a warm reception from local law enforcement. Sometimes they feel like we are interfering." Regan interjected.

"Always one to do my part for the government. Ever since WW2. Proud to serve." Andrews said.

"Where were you in the war?" Regan asked.

"I was with the Big Red One. Rolling across France." Andrews said proudly.

"Must have seen a lot of action." Regan said.

Andrews hesitated. "Yeah. Some. Truth is I drove the big deuces. Supply trucks."

"A critical part of any operation." Regan said nodding.

"Course that was nothing like this spider business." Andrews said.

"So maybe you could bring us up to speed on exactly what went on out here." Simms said.

"Sure. Sure I can." Andrews said. "Well, you see, it's like this. This Professor Deemer and a couple of his assistants, well, they were working on a drug of some kind. Guess it was supposed to grow things bigger. Animals, not people. It didn't work on people. It gave people some disease. A disease that deformed them. Both of Deemer's assistants died from trying to use the serum on themselves."

"Why would they try it on themselves?" Simms asked.

Andrews shrugged. "I don't know. Those scientist types are crazy dedicated to their work. Anyway, this drug, it worked on animals. Made them grow big."

Simms glanced over at Regan. There was an unspoken question between them. It sounded similar to a story from the beginning of the OSO years ago.

"Go on." Simms said.

Andrews nodded. "Well, it seems that there was an accident at the Professor's lab and one of his animals, a tarantula, got out. And, you know what? That thing just kept on growing. It killed some cattle. Cleaned them right down to the bone. Then it got some of our local folk as well. It killed Professor Deemer too. Probably would have destroyed the whole town if the State Police hadn't called in the Air Force to blow it up."

Beka made a sound. They glanced over at her.

"I hate spiders." Beka said.

"Well, most people do, but everybody hates giant ones." Andrews said.

"So you are certain that it is dead?" Regan asked.

Andrews nodded emphatically. "Absolutely sure. I watched the Air Force burn it up with napalm. You can see the burnt up remains just outside of town."

"And that's the only specimen to escape Deemer's lab?" Simms asked.

Andrews shrugged. "Haven't been any sign of anything else."

The sun was setting and the last rays streamed into the passenger side windows. The air outside was beginning its nightly cooling. Ahead they could see the lights of Desert Rock drawing closer. A short time later they pulled into town and stopped in front of the Sheriff's office.

Hastings and Steve had been sitting on a bench in the park across the street from the Sheriff's office. They hustled over to the Sheriff's car.

Hastings grabbed a hold of Andrews arm. "Jack, there's another one."

Steve nodded anxiously. "Just as big as the first."

Andrews hesitated. His brain was trying to process what they were telling him and he didn't want to believe it.

"Are you sure?" Andrews asked.

"Sure enough that it nearly brought Andy's barn down on top of us." Hastings said.

Andrews turned to Simms and Regan. "Uh, these men are from the SS...O..."

"The OSO." Simms said stepping forward. "The Office of Scientific Operations."

Hastings looked at Simms, then Andrews, then back again at Simms. "The...Office...I'm sorry I don't know what that is."

"We're a monster hunting team." Beka said.

"Not a team. And...we do much more than just hunt monsters." Simms said.

"But mainly we hunt monsters." Regan added.

"Anyway, I am Agent Simms and this is Agent Regan." Simms turned and gestured towards Regan.

"I'm Beka." Beka stepped forward and shook Steve and Hastings hands.

Hastings slowly shook Beka's hand, clearly confused.

"Why don't you tell us what happened." Simms said.

Hastings told them about Brian's arrival in town and their subsequent trip out to Andy's ranch.

"Was it headed this way?" Andrews asked.

Hastings shook his head. "Not when we last saw it."

"So, the Air Force was able to neutralize this giant spider with fighter jets out of Sands?" Simms asked.

"Yes." Hastings nodded. "They used napalm on it."

"OK." Simms said looking at the skies around them. "Well, there's no way the pilots are going to be able to spot a black spider in the dark. Even a giant one. I will call Sands and gets some planes out here first thing in the morning."

"If you need help convincing the Air Force to send out the planes, Lieutenant Nolan of the State Police has friends over there." Andrews offered.

Simms graced Andrews with a friendly smile. "I...won't have trouble getting the planes. Thank you."

"We have connections in high places." Beka said.

Simms sighed. "There's no *we* here."

"I would suggest you make sure the townspeople stay indoors for tonight." Regan suggested.

Andrews nodded. "Yes, of course. I'll get some men together and get the word out."

"Sheriff, if I could use your phone..." Simms said.

Andrews had turned to move down the street, but stopped. "Of course. This way."

Simms turned to Regan. "Maybe you should get us a couple of rooms." He waved a hand towards the Palace Hotel just down the street.

Regan nodded. "Sure."

Simms followed Andrews into the office. Regan and Beka walked down the street and into the Palace Hotel.

"Evening." Regan said to the hotel manager.

The hotel manager looked up from his comic book. He was an older man in a white shirt and suspenders.

"Evening, sir. You and the missus need a room?" The hotel manager asked.

"Oh, uh, we're not..." Regan stammered.

"We're government agents. Here about the monster." Beka said.

"Oh, heard you folks was coming." The hotel manager said.

Regan glanced at Beka and then to the hotel manager. "Uh, two rooms."

The hotel watched them for a moment. "Cheaper if you just get one room." He said with a small smirk.

"Our other team member needs a room as well." Beka said.

Regan opened his mouth to say something and then clearly changed his mind about what he was going to say. He looked at Beka. "Is there any point in my saying anything?"

Beka shrugged. "No. Not really."

"I thought not." Regan said. He looked at the hotel manager. "I guess it's been kind of exciting around here lately."

The hotel manager turned and grabbed a couple of keys. He turned back to Regan. "You can say that again. A little too exciting for me. Been planning my retirement, but I'm thinking of moving my plans up a little."

"Are you going to stay here in Desert Rock?" Beka asked.

The hotel manager frowned at Beka. "Heck no. I have had enough of the desert. I'm going to move up north. Going to move to the family farm."

"Oh, where's that?" Beka asked as she signed the hotel register next to Regan's name.

"A small town called Hooterville." The hotel manager said.

"Huh, sounds nice. A little place of your own out in the country. A few green acres." Beka said with a smile.

5

The morning sun streamed across the desert. Simms, Regan, Beka and Andrews stood out in the street in front of the Sheriff's Office scanning the skies above. They could hear the planes in the distance, but were having trouble spotting them in the vast blue sky.

"That's not a jet fighter." Andrews said.

"Those are reconn planes." Simms said. "They are just searching for the spider. When they spot it they will call in the fighters."

"Oh, I understand." Andrews said.

They stood watching for a little while as the planes crisscrossed the sky working in some kind of pattern. As they waited Hastings eventually joined them. Other people popped out of various buildings and houses around the town and watched the planes.

Steve emerged from the hotel and joined the others.

"Have they killed it yet?" Steve asked.

"No. I don't think they have found it as yet." Regan answered.

"How can they not find it? It was as big as that barn." Steve commented.

Regan glanced at Simms. They both knew that if the spider was anywhere within 10 miles of the town the planes should have spotted it by now. Something seemed odd. They didn't doubt the word of these people about what they had seen, but, if the spider was still around and as big as they said it was, the reconn planes should have seen it by this point in time.

"Well, they'll just have to keep expanding the search pattern until they spot it." Simms said. "In the meantime, I guess maybe we could take a look at what is left of Deemer's lab."

Andrews looked at Simms. "Sure. I can take you out there."

"I would like to go back out there as well." Steve said.

Hastings looked at Steve. He wasn't sure why she would want to go back out. He suspected she was hoping to find more of Deemer's lost notes. More than just the couple of notebooks she was able to pull out of the rubble yesterday.

"I guess you can count me in as well." Hastings said.

"Great. When do we leave?" Beka asked.

Simms turned towards Beka. "You are staying here."

Beka stared at Simms defiantly.

Regan stepped close to Beka. "Please stay here."

"Why? She's going." Beka waved at Steve.

"She's a scientist. And she's seen this creature before. And...well, that thing might...be there." Regan said.

Beka looked hard at Regan and then her eyes softened. "You're going out there."

"It's what I do." Regan said.

Beka sighed. "Damn it. OK. I'll just sit here like a good girl."

"Thank you." Regan said.

The five of them squeezed into Andrews' squad car. As they drove off west towards the ruins of Deemer's house Beka stood on the sidewalk and watched them go.

The car pulled up in front of the remains of Deemer's house. Simms and Regan stared at the destroyed house while the other three cautiously scanned around in all directions.

"Well, that's a thorough job of ripping a house apart." Regan said.

"It is." Simms said nodding.

"I don't see any sign of it." Hastings said quietly as he stood next to Andrews.

The Sheriff had instinctively put a hand on his revolver in its holster. "Me either." Andrews said.

Simms turned towards Steve. "Did Deemer ever mention that his work was based on anyone else's?"

Steve shook her head. "I don't recall him saying anything like that."

"How fast did the test animals respond to the drug?" Simms asked.

"It was not instantaneous, if that's what you are asking." Steve replied. "It typically took multiple shots to complete the whole series."

"So, it took some time for the animal to respond." Simms said.

Steve stepped past Simms and a little ways into the wreckage. "Oh, there were noticeable changes within 24 hours, but significant growth took place only after about the sixth injection."

Simms followed Steve into the mess. "But the subjects couldn't have gotten as big as these tarantulas are now while still here at the lab."

Steve glanced back at Simms. "Oh, no. The largest the tarantula got here in the lab was about the size of a cat."

Simms noticed that Steve seemed to be deliberately moving towards a particular part of the house. He continued following her. "So, the tarantula continued to grow after it escaped the lab."

Steve nodded. "It seems so."

"That would suggest a problem with the serum." Simms said.

Steve stopped and quickly turned around to look at Simms. "What do you mean?"

"Well, if Deemer's goal was to increase the size of animals for the purposes of food production it would have been impractical to try to feed or contain animals as large as these tarantulas have gotten to." Simms said.

Steve shook her head. "No. The animals would simply need to be harvested before they reached that size."

"Maybe." Simms said. "I can't imagine how one would go about killing or butchering a forty foot tall steer."

"I am sure some enterprising people will figure it out." Steve said as she started poking around under some broken boards in a corner.

"Looking for something?" Simms asked her.

Steve quickly stood up. "No. Nothing."

"Did any of Deemer's notes survive?" Simms asked.

Steve hesitated. "Sadly no."

"So all of his work is lost then?" Simms asked. He slid some pieces of shattered equipment around with his foot.

"I'm afraid so." Steve said without looking at Simms.

Regan made his way through the rubble to Simms. "The doctor says he and Miss Clayton here thought they saw something when they were out here the other day. Just on the other side of that hill."

Simms nodded. "Guess it's worth a look."

Simms and Regan clambered out through the back of the building. They were joined by Andrews. The three of them slowly worked their way up the hillside. As they neared the top Simms and Regan noticed the Sheriff had pulled out his revolver. They exchanged a look. Without saying anything they pulled their guns out as well. Every OSO agent was issued a .45, though, truth be told, they were rarely effective weapons against the kind of creatures the agents typically encountered.

The infectious caution of Andrews made all three of them slow as they crested the top of the ridge. They looked down into the flat desert on the other side. Nothing. Just desert. They scanned in all directions from the height of the ridge, but there seemed to be nothing stirring as far they could see.

Regan pointed out into the distance. "Our reconn planes."

Simms shaded his eyes and followed Regan's extended arm. "Still searching."

"You think it has moved off?" Regan asked.

Simms shrugged. "Maybe. If that's what happened, though, we will probably hear about it soon enough. Something that big will have a pretty hefty appetite."

"Still, the planes are covering a wider and wider area. You'd think they would spot it traveling somewhere." Regan said.

"Agreed." Simms said.

"Maybe it's just hiding somewhere." Andrews volunteered.

"Where do you hide a spider three stories tall?" Regan asked.

Down in the lab area of what used to be Deemer's house Steve wrestled with a crushed workbench.

"Help me with this." Steve said to Hastings who hovered nearby.

Hastings stepped carefully over to her and helped her slide back some pieces of wood. "Are you still looking for more of Deemer's journals?"

Steve glanced at Hastings. "Of course. I'm sure there are more somewhere. I know there is at least one notebook I was entering data in that is in here someplace."

"Steve, I really think you should tell the government guys about Deemer's notes." Hastings said tentatively. He was pretty sure what her reaction would be.

Steve gave him a sharp look. "They are from the government." She said the word government like it was an enemy.

"Right. And they would have the resources to safely develop Deemer's work." Hastings said.

"The government has a long history of just taking the hard work of scientists. They think everything is theirs for the taking in the name of national security." Steve said.

Hastings shrugged. "I don't know."

"I do know. They did it to my father. He had spent years improving crop yields before the government came along and took it from him. Told him his work was meant to benefit everyone. As if he was going to withhold it from people or something. And they have the nerve to tell us to worry about the Communists." Steve's voice rose somewhat.

"OK. OK. I won't say anything to them about it, but everybody in the government isn't bad." Hastings said.

Steve said nothing and continued pushed debris around. She made a sound and snatched up a notebook.

"Find something?" Hastings asked.

"One of my notebooks." Steve said. She slid it into her purse.

By the time the others had returned from the ridge top Hastings and Steve had worked their way back out of the house. They agreed there wasn't anything more to see here and climbed back into the car. Moments later they were heading back towards Desert Rock.

6

After the others had driven away Beka stood for a couple minutes unsure what to do. Desert rock was a pretty small town and she was sure she would find little of interest in such a quiet and sleepy place.

She began strolling slowly along the sidewalk. As she passed the Sheriff's office a sad chugging sound grew louder next to her. She stopped and watched an old car pull up to the curb. An old weathered man climbed out and walked towards the Sheriff's office.

"The sheriff's not there." Beka said to the man.

The old man stopped. He hesitated. He looked in the window of the office and then back at Beka.

"Where's the Sheriff?" The old man said. "I need to talk to the Sheriff."

"He's gone out to...well, somewhere." Beka thought for a moment. "Maybe I can help you."

The old man stared at her briefly. "You?"

Beka stepped up to the man. She extended her hand. The old man slowly took her hand.

"I'm Beka Woods. Government Agent with the OSO." Beka said.

The man stared at her for almost a full minute. "Government agent?"

"Yes sir. The Office of Scientific Operations. We hunt monsters." Beka said proudly.

"You do?" The old man's eyes widened. "Then you must be here cause of them big spiders."

Beka nodded. "Yup. That's why we're here. So what can I help you with?"

The old man looked up and down her. "I ain't never seen a woman G-Man before. Didn't know they came as women now days. Dang it, things sure are a changing."

"Yes, they are." Beka said. "So, what do you need the Sheriff for?"

"Well, it's my wife..." The old man said.

Beka frowned at the man. "I told you we hunt monsters. No matter what you may think of your wife—-"

The old man waved off Beka's words. "No. No. My wife is missing."

"Oh. OK. Maybe you should tell me what happened." Beka said.

"Well, early this morning she went out to feed the chickens and, well, she was just gone. She never came back in so I went out looking for her and she wasn't nowhere." The old man said.

Beka thought for a moment. "OK. Well, maybe you should show me where this happened."

The old man nodded solemnly. "I can take you out there."

Beka waved him on and the two of them climbed into his car. With a rough coughing the car came back to life, though for a moment Beka wasn't sure it would. They drove out of town to the east. The old man did not drive fast and Beka was sure that if she had been driving they would have made it to the old man's farm in half the time.

It was a small farm in an open area of the desert. A cozy house, a larger building that seemed to serve as both a barn and a workshop and a chicken coop. There were a couple of larger trees around the place that obviously were getting watered by the farmer and his wife. The chickens congregated under the shade of the trees.

Beka and the old man got out of the car.

“So, you wife was just out here somewhere feeding the chickens and then she was gone?” Beka asked waving towards the trees.

The old man thought for a minute. “No. I doubt she would have been there. The chickens don’t go under the trees until the sun gets hot. She would have been by the coop this morning.”

The old man shuffled over to the chicken coop and stood there not really seeming to know what to do next. Beka joined him standing next to rickety wood frame of the coop. She looked around, but saw nothing of interest.

Beka looked further out across the sandy yard. “What’s that?” She pointed out past the immediate area of the farm.

The old man followed Beka out among some small scrubby bushes. At first Beka thought perhaps it was the prone figure of the missing wife, though, admittedly the old man's wife would have to have been a small woman, but as they drew closer Beka saw that it was just a burlap sack.

"It's the feed bag." The old man said as picked it up. The bag was still half full of seed. "This is what we use to feed the chickens."

"What's it doing out here?" Beka asked.

The old man pushed his wide brimmed hat back a little. "I don't know."

"Do you think your wife might have run off somewhere?" Beka asked.

The old man gave her a funny look. "Now why would she want to leave a fine place like this?"

Beka scanned the aging farm. She could think of a great many reasons to run away from this place. "I'm sure I don't know."

The old man stared at the seed bag. "Don't make no sense."

Beka looked off into the distance. She saw, just beyond a small rise in the distance an isolated could of sand and dust. "What's that?"

The old man followed where Beka pointed at the dust could.

"They call 'em Dust Devils around here. The wind stirs up some of the sand. That's a kind of small one. Don't see them very often here. At least, till recently. Been seein' them more often." The old man explained.

Beka sighed. "Well, I don't know. I guess we better get back into town and let the Sheriff know about your wife. Maybe he has some ideas."

The old man shrugged. They walked back to the car and Beka endured another unhurried drive back into town.

As they pulled up to the curb in front of the Sheriff's office and got out, Beka turned to see the others returning from their trip to Deemer's house. She waited on the sidewalk for everyone to climb out of the Sheriff's car.

Regan looked at the old man, his car and then Beka. "Apparently you managed to stay busy while we were gone."

Beka saluted. "An OSO agents job is never done."

"OK. Now I'm worried." Regan said.

Beka indicated the old man. "It seems his wife has gone missing."

"Well, it isn't the most exciting place to live. Maybe..." Regan gave a small shrug.

"That's what I thought, but he insists she wouldn't just run off." Beka said.

The old man quickly scuffled over to Andrews.

"Bailey." Andrews said in greeting.

"Sheriff, my Ella, she's gone missing." Bailey said.

"Missing?" Andrews stared at Bailey for a moment. His mind was on bigger issues and he had to refocus.

"Yeah. She went to feed the chickens and then she was gone." Bailey said.

"Hmm. Sure she didn't just go off to visit family or something?" Andrews asked.

Bailey shook his head. "Not without the car."

"Oh, guess so." Andrews said. "Well, I guess I could come out and take a look around."

"The government woman already did that." Bailey said.

Simms, who had been hovering nearby, stepped over. He spoke before Andrews could answer Bailey.

"Government woman?" Simms looked directly at Bailey.

Bailey waved at Beka, but Simms already knew who he was referring to. Simms turned slowly and stared at Beka.

Beka flashed Simms a small friendly smile. She held up a hand as Simms walked over to her. "I know what you are going to say, but I was just trying to help out. You know, gather some more information."

Simms stared straight at Beka. "Impersonating a Federal Agent is a crime."

"I was just trying to be useful. You know, since I was just left behind." Beka said. She was starting to get upset and it surprised her. She hadn't realized that after years of drifting along in life she found that being a part of something, this particular something, really meant something to her.

Simms opened his mouth to say something, but Regan reached out and put a hand on Simms shoulder. He gently pulled Simms back a step and stepped in front of Beka. The move surprised Simms. He said nothing and stared at Regan.

"Beka, what would have happened if the giant spider had been there?" Regan looked closely at her.

"I...uh..." Beka's eyes cast about.

Simms shifted uncomfortably. He was so focused on being pissed at Beka for pushing the idea that she was an OSO agent it hadn't actually occurred to him the danger she had put herself in. Simms was still pissed, but more at how he felt like he had lost sight of his primary purpose which was to protect people. Everybody. Even Beka. He had lost sight of that. He took a deep breath.

"Elliot and I have trained for this and have been through all kinds of dangers. It's what we do." Regan said.

"I know. I know." Beka said lowering her head. "I'm sorry. I guess, I just wanted help and...I didn't think about it."

Simms watched Beka for a moment more. He could see she genuinely wanted to help them. At that moment Simms remembered something Regan had told him back in San Francisco just after they had rescued Beka. She had no where else to go. She was a loner—-just like they were. It was kind of a prerequisite for being an OSO agent.

Simms stepped up next to Regan. "Next time, check with us before just running off. It's what we are always careful to do." Simms indicated he was referring to how he and Regan work.

Regan took a half step back. He wasn't sure he heard Simms correctly. Did he just make it sound like Beka was on the "team"?

Beka lifted her head. She wiped the trace of a tear away. She gave Simms and Regan a small smile. "I will. I promise."

"Did you see anything of interest at the old man's place?" Simms asked.

Beka's smile broadened. It almost seemed like she was going to hug Simms, but instead she answered him as if she was giving a report.

"Nothing unusual. No sign of any kind of struggle. Just the bag of chicken feed she had was found a short ways away from the yard where the chickens were." Beka said.

Simms thought about that for a moment. He nodded and turned back towards the Sheriff.

"Sheriff Andrews, given that we have another creature out there somewhere it's probably prudent to follow up on anything out of the ordinary." Simms said.

Andrews nodded in agreement. "OK." He turned back to Bailey and started asking him a few more questions.

Regan, Beka and Simms walked over next the Andrews.

"So you haven't noticed anything else odd happening out there?" Andrews asked.

Bailey shook his head slowly. "No. Nothing I can think of."

"Oh, there was the Dust Devil." Beka said.

"Oh, that." Bailey said. "Yeah, I've seen quite a few of those lately. Guess that is a little odd."

Andrews nodded. "Yeah. A number of people have mentioned that."

"Dust Devil?" Regan asked.

Andrews explained what it was.

A plane few overhead. Everyone looked up at it.

"If you don't mind Sheriff, I going to use your phone again. I don't understand why they haven't spotted the thing yet." Simms said.

"Doesn't make any sense." Regan agreed.

7

The five of them sat around the table at the restaurant. Hastings sat next to Steve. Beka, Regan and Simms completed the circle. The sun had just set behind some hills to the north. The conversation had been pleasant small talk.

Beka had just commented on the heat of the desert sun when Steve changed the subject abruptly.

"So, you seem very interested in Professor Deemer's work." Steve said turning slightly to her left to look at Simms. Hastings shifted uncomfortably in his seat. He knew what was on Steve's mind.

Simms gave a slight shrug. "Possibly. We have seen similar work as this in other places."

"That sounds interesting." Hastings said quickly. "Maybe you could tell us about that."

"Are you saying Professor Deemer's work is plagiarized from someone else?" Steve asked, sounding offended.

Simms shook his head. "Not necessarily, but he may have come across other work of a similar nature."

"He didn't say anything to me about anyone else's work." Steve said. She gave Hastings a quick glance. Hastings knew she took Simms' words as proof that the government was intent upon taking Deemer's work.

"We would like to analyze his research work. It might to point to clues about a body of work that has been lost." Simms said.

Steve waved off Simms' words. "You can call it analyzing, the truth is it's just a way to seize scientific research for military use."

There was an awkward pause around the table.

"That's probably not quite the way to phrase that." Hastings said.

"The OSO doesn't *seize* scientific research. That's not our job. Our job is to protect people from danger whether it is of natural or man made origin." Regan said.

"I'm sure that's not exactly what Steve meant." Hastings said.

"No, that's pretty much what I meant." Steve said.

Simms studied Steve for a moment. He knew there was a portion of the scientific community that felt like Steve did, but he was not interested in debating the validity of such paranoia. He sighed.

"My partner is correct. The OSO does not seize scientific research and we are certainly not here for that purpose. Our interest in Deemer's work is related to a longstanding investigation by the OSO in some research work from the past that has gone missing." Simms said. He waved a hand dismissively. "In this case, since Deemer's notes were lost the entire issue is moot."

Steve said nothing and stared down at the cup of coffee in front of her.

Simms watched out of the corner of his eye. He suspected now that Deemer's work was not, in fact, lost.

Hastings looked at Steve, but said nothing. He could tell she didn't believe what Agent Simms was telling her.

"Are you leaving Desert Rock now that Professor Deemer's work here is done?" Beka asked, looking at Steve.

Steve look up from her cup. She gave a quick glance around the table and then back to Beka. "I believe I will stay on here for a little while. I would like to get some biological samples from this second tarantula. If the Air Force leaves me anything to get a sample from."

The conversation drifted for a few more minutes before Beka sighed.

"I think it feels a little stuffy in here. I think I'd like to get a little fresh air." Beka said, looking at Regan.

Regan nodded. "OK. Sounds good to me."

"I think that would do everyone some good." Hastings said standing up with Beka and Regan.

Simms and Steve also stood up from the table and the five of them made their way out on to the sidewalk. Darkness had settled in and the air had noticeably cooled. Beka hooked arms with Regan and Steve did the same with Hastings. Slowly they all started walking along the sidewalk.

After a couple of minutes of walking the group suddenly stopped in their tracks as all of the lights of Desert Rock went out. A moment passed and the lights started coming back on.

"Well, that was strange." Beka said.

Regan glanced back at Simms and they exchanged a look of mild concern.

"Oh, that's nothing." Hastings said. "It happens regularly out here. Something will happen to one of the power lines coming into town, but it comes back on. The power line runs from Sandy Flats to the east through Desert Rock and on to Red Cliffs west of here. If we lose power from one direction, after a minute, we just get power fed back to us from the other direction."

"So...something took out the power line in one of the directions?" Regan asked.

"Sure. Like I said it..." Hastings said, stopping in mid sentence.

Everyone exchanged a look. It occurred to all of them that this quite possibly wasn't a typical power outage.

"Uh, maybe we should check the power lines east and west of here." Simms said.

"That's not going to be very easy in the dark." Hastings said.

"We should be able to see if a power line is still up with flashlights." Regan said.

"Right." Simms agreed.

"I guess." Hastings said. "I'll go get the Sheriff and I guess we could just split up. One group go west and the other east."

"That's what I was thinking." Simms nodded.

"So what do I do?" Beka asked.

Simms looked at her. "Well, if we find something we'll call it in when we can get to a phone."

"Well, look at it this way," Regan said smiling, "while we're out there the spider might come right here into town and you'll have it all to yourself."

"Funny." Beka said sarcastically. "I did mention I hate spiders, right?"

It didn't take Hastings long to find Andrews and within a few minutes they were headed out of town west, towards Red Cliffs. It was slow going spotting the thin power lines in the dark with a flashlight, but the longer they were at it, the better they got at recognizing that the line was still up.

"Hold up here." Hastings said pulling his head back into the car.

"You see something?" Andrews asked. There was a slight tinge of fear in his voice. The previous tarantula had thrown a pickup truck off the road and down an embankment. In then proceeded to eat the occupants.

"No. The lines went up the slope there and I can't see them from here. I just want to get out and double check." Hastings said.

Andrews stopped the car. Hastings got out and took a couple of steps off the road shining his flashlight up a sandy slope towards the power lines. Andrews opened his door and stood just outside the door of the car.

"You see 'em?" Andrews called out.

"Yeah. They're still up there. Wait! Did you hear that?" Hastings froze where he stood.

"Hear what?" Andrews asked.

"Shh!" Hastings stared out into the darkness and waved a hand back at Andrews to quiet him. He shot the light of the flashlight left and right and back again.

Andrews wasn't sure if Hastings was just imagining something, but then he heard it too. It was a strong and yet oddly soft thumping sound. A couple of thumps and then silence. After about thirty seconds another couple of thumps, but no clear sense of where it was coming from.

Hastings turned around and looked at Andrews. He didn't say anything, but there was a question in his eyes. Andrews looked back at Hastings and shrugged. The sound seemed to stop.

Hastings walked slowly back to the car. He stood next to it still listening.

"That...didn't sound like any of the sounds we heard from the other tarantula." Hastings said.

Andrews nodded and then shook his head as if he was agreeing and disagreeing. "Yeah. I don't remember anything like that before."

After another full minute of listening to the silent desert and an exchange of looks the two of them climbed back into car. Andrews drove on. Hastings leaned out the car window as he continued to try to track the power lines.

They drove for while and were able to move a little faster as the power lines came closer to the road. Eventually the road climbed a slow steady rise for a mile. As they reached the top Andrews slowed to a stop.

Hastings pulled his head back in the window. "What's wrong?" He asked looking over at Andrews.

Andrews pointed out into the distance a little to the left. Hastings looked out and saw a glow on the horizon.

"Red Cliffs." Andrews said.

"Oh." Hastings said with a short nod. "They have electricity. I guess the lines aren't down between here and there."

Andrews nodded. "Right." He turned the car around and began heading back towards Desert Rock.

"Well," Hastings said sitting back in the seat, "maybe our government agents are having better luck."

"If you want to call it that." Andrews said.

Hastings glanced over at Andrews. It took him a moment to catch Andrews' meaning.

"Oh, yeah, like finding a giant tarantula on a lonely dark road." Hastings said.

"Exactly." Andrews said emphatically.

8

"You know you can drive faster." Regan said pulling his head back inside the car. "I can see the lines pretty good from here."

Simms glanced over at Regan. "I wasn't driving slower so you could see better. I...didn't want to run into anything."

Regan looked over at Simms. "It's a flat straight road in the desert. What were you thinking you were going to run into?"

"A large black leg." Simms said staring straight ahead.

"Oh." Regan said. "Right."

They drove for a little while through the dark in silence.

"I guess you better pull over here." Regan finally said.

"Really?" Simms asked. "We just stopped fifteen minutes ago."

"No. Not to pee. The poles are a little further out here and I can't tell if they're up or not." Regan said.

"Oh. OK." Simms pulled the car over on to the shoulder of the road. Regan slid out of the passenger side and took a few steps out towards the dark desert. He waved the flashlight around and stopped on something. Simms couldn't tell what Regan was focused on. Instinctively he moved his hand to the .45 in his shoulder holster.

Regan turned and walked back to the car. "The lines are still up here." He climbed back into the car.

Simms drove on further down the road.

"What's that?" Regan said as Simms was slowing down.

"Not sure...wait...it's sparks." Simms slowed to a stop. They got out of the car and stared at flickering lights and that seemed to dance a little around on the pavement about twenty feet in front of them.

"Well, I guess that's our downed power line." Regan said.

"Yeah." Simms said. He shone a second flashlight around into the black shrouded desert night.

"Whoa." Regan said.

Simms turned around and followed the beam of Regan's flashlight. He saw the wooden pole that held the power line. It was push over at about a 45 degree angle.

"Something hit that." Regan commented.

"Looks like it." Simms agreed.

Regan scanned the darkness with his flashlight, but saw nothing. A moment later he froze. There was a distinct sound of rocks colliding. He could just make out a low ridge about 80 feet in front of him.

"Did you hear that?" Regan asked.

"I heard something." Simms said shining his flashlight past Regan towards the sound.

They both stood silently for a moment. The sound came again and it was clearly something moving, but they couldn't see what it was. It did, however, seemed to be getting closer.

Both of them drew their guns out. Regan wasn't sure he could anything, but the sound suggested a direction. He took aim and fired off a couple of shots.

"See something?" Simms asked.

Regan shook his head. "Not really, but something is there."

"Maybe it would be prudent for us to back away. The Sheriff did say ordinary bullets didn't seem to significantly affect that thing." Simms said.

Regan back to the car and climbed back in as Simms slid behind the wheel. Simms started the car and, while Regan carefully watched in the direction of the sounds they had heard, Simms turned the car around. Slowly Simms drove away.

Regan turned around to look out the back window. It was a very limited view since the taillights emitted only a dim light in their wake. Suddenly, the car swerved and Regan banged backwards into the passenger door.

"What the hell...?" Regan exclaimed.

"Sorry. Something in the road." Simms said.

"What was it?" Regan asked.

"Not sure." Simms said concentrating on the road in front of them.

"You must have seen something. You swerved pretty hard." Regan said.

Simms shook his head slightly. "Don't know. It was more like I lost sight of the road. Like it just disappeared."

"Well, you must have—-oh shit!" Regan said. A large black column suddenly appeared in the middle of the road directly in front of them. Again Simms yanked the wheel and the car dove to one side barely missing the black thing in the road.

"It looked like that." Simms said.

"Yeah. I figured that out." Regan said.

"I have a feeling that was—-" Simms started saying when there came a loud bang on the roof of the car. The middle part of the car roof buckle in some. Both Simms and Regan instinctively ducked their heads.

"Yeah. I think we both have a feeling for what that was." Regan said.

A second bang struck the roof and this time about ten inches of something pointed and black penetrated through the roof between the two of them. A moment later the pointed thing disappeared.

Simms stomped on the accelerator. The car took off.

"Can we out run it?" Regan asked.

"We'll find out." Simms said.

"That's a hell of a lot bigger than a giant ant." Regan said.

"Definitely." Simms said.

A moment later another black column appeared in the road ahead. They both now knew it was a leg of the tarantula.

"I don't think we're out running it." Regan said.

"No. We're not." Simms said. He swerved around the leg and his eyes darted back and forth at the terrain on either side of the road. On an impulse Simms yanked the wheel to the right. The tires squealed and the car fish tailed some, but then dropped off the road and down a small slope.

"This car isn't that good on the pavement. It's not going to be any better in the sand." Regan said.

"I know." Simms said as he slammed on the brakes. Regan bounced into the dashboard.

"Hey!" Regan said.

"Get out! Now!" Simms yelled and swung his door open.

"What?" Regan asked, but he flung his door open anyway.

"This way!" Simms said as he ran back towards the road. He fired off a couple of shots in the general direction of the road as he went.

Regan followed him. As he rounded the car he saw where Simms was going. There was a culvert that ran under the road here. It allowed the flash flood water that would occasionally run through the wash they were now in to run under the road.

Simms scrambled into the four foot high culvert and Regan followed him in. They sat inside the culvert breathing heavily with their guns ready. They could hear some thumping around outside of the culvert, but it was impossible from where they were to determine where the sounds were coming from.

The smashing of metal and shattering of glass told them that the tarantula was destroying the car. They listened to the car being crushed for a couple of minutes and then it was quiet.

"Damn." Simms said.

"Yeah." Regan said. "That's going to look bad on the expense report."

"Right." Simms said.

It grew quiet for a couple of minutes.

"So, do we have a plan?" Regan asked.

"I'm working on it." Simms said.

There was a scuffling clunk at the entrance to the culvert, a few feet away from Regan.

"What was that?" Regan asked swiveling the flashlight around towards the opening of the culvert. Regan stared at the end of the culvert. His eyes were fooling him. The flashlight shone at what he knew was the opening of the culvert, but all he could see was blackness. The blackness moved.

"Shit." Regan said and shuffled to his left running into Simms.

"What? What's going on?" Simms asked.

"The damned thing is trying to reach into the culvert with a leg." Regan explained.

Simms shifted several feet to his left in the direction of the other opening on the other side of the road. Regan shifted with him to put more distance between himself and the black leg that was poking into the culvert.

The tarantula's leg withdrew. Both watched the end of the culvert to see if the leg reappeared. It didn't. Minutes passed. Simms heard something and realized the sound was coming from his left. He turned and shone his flashlight at the other end of the culvert which was only about six feet to his left. He could make out the light colored sand of the wash just beyond the opening and then it disappeared. There was nothing but blackness.

"Damn. It's over here now." Simms slid to his right running into Regan.

"Smart bastard." Regan said. "I guess maybe we should try to stay in the middle."

"Yeah. I don't think it can reach very far into here." Simms said.

After the black leg poked around several feet into the culvert for another minute it withdrew. They sat quietly. They could hear some scuffling around outside, but there were no more attempts to reach into the culvert. It grew quiet.

"Well this is going to be a long night." Regan said trying to relieve the pain in his butt from the ribbed metal of the culvert.

"At least when it gets light out there we'll be able to spot it from a distance." Simms said.

"Maybe, but I don't see us out running it." Regan commented.

"No. I doubt that, but someone will be out looking for us by then." Simms said.

"Yeah, if they don't find that creature first. I wish we could get word to them that it's here. I don't want them just driving right into it." Regan said.

Simms glanced over in the direction of Regan's voice. Their flashlights were off and it was very dark in the culvert. He couldn't help thinking that Regan was specifically worried about Beka driving out looking for them and encountering the spider.

"Well, unless that thing heads into town it's more likely to wander off into the desert." Simms said.

"I suppose so." Regan said.

They were quiet again for a few minutes. Finally Regan spoke up.

"You realize that if the planes can't spot that thing we're going to need a plan B."

Simms nodded even though Regan couldn't see him. "I know. Been thinking about that. Whatever plan B is though, it's going to have to involve more firepower than our pistols."

"That's for damn sure." Regan agreed.

The two of them hunkered down for a bruising night in the cramped culvert.

9

Beka's eyes flickered. She stared, unseeing, around the room. Things didn't seem to be in focus and she thought at first that she was still dreaming. As she took a deep breath and opened hers eyes a little wider she realized that part of the dreamlike feel to her surroundings was the dim gray light that cascaded throughout the room from the window.

Beka's thoughts started coming together. She was slouching in an armchair in the hotel room she was sharing with Robbie. Robbie? Beka scanned around the room, the bed in particular. No Robbie.

Beka sat up in the chair and digested the situation for a moment more. She looked over at the window. It was almost dawn. Why didn't Robbie wake her when he came in? Why did he come in and then leave again? Wait. Maybe he never came in.

Beka stood up. She looked down at herself. She was still wearing yesterday's clothes. Something was going on. Or something was wrong. Beka started towards the door and then, as an afterthought, ducked her head into the bathroom. No Robbie.

In the hallway Beka hesitated. She had to think for a moment to remember which room Elliot was in. She walked quickly two doors down the hall and banged on the door. No answer. She banged again. Nothing.

Turning she went down the stairs to the front desk. The old man was, as always, sitting in a chair behind the desk reading something.

"Where's Robbie?" Beka asked.

The hotel manager looked up from what he was reading. "Robbie?"

"Yes. Agent Regan." Beka said impatiently.

"Oh, one of the government guys. Don't know." The manager said.

"I...don't think he came back to the room." Beka said.

The hotel manager stared back at Beka. He seemed to not know what he should say to that.

Beka focused her thoughts. "Did you see either of the government men come in during the night."

The hotel manager shook his head. "No one came in here during the night. Leastwise not that I saw."

Beka stood for a moment thinking. The Sheriff. He and the doctor were out following the power lines too. Were they back?

Beka walked out of the hotel and over to the Sheriff's office. There was no one stirring about the town this early. The townspeople had been warned to stay indoors as much as possible. Beka was about to bang on the door of the Sheriff's office when she tried the door knob. It opened.

Inside Beka found the Sheriff asleep in his desk chair. No one else was there. She circled the desk and shook the Sheriff's shoulder.

"What? What is it?" Andrews said looking left and right, but not really seeing anything.

"Where are the two government men?" Beka asked.

"The two what?" Andrews turned and looked at Beka like she was a complete stranger.

"The two government men. Agent Regan and Agent Simms. Where are they?" Beka asked.

Andrews looked around the room as if he was trying to spot them. "I...don't know. I...was waiting for them to get here. Must have fallen asleep. What time is it?"

Beka glanced at the clock on the wall. "Just about 6."

Andrews thought for a moment. "They should have been back by now."

"Yes. So we need to go look for them." Beka said.

"Right. Right." Andrews stood up. "Right. Let's take a ride."

The two of them walked out of the office. Out on the street they saw Hastings approaching.

"Do you know where the government guys are?" Andrews asked Hastings as he walked up.

Hastings shook his head. "No. I was wondering if they found anything. I couldn't really sleep so I decided to see if they were here."

"We were just going out to look for them." Beka said.

"I think we better do that." Hastings said.

They climbed into the Sheriff's car and headed out of town. They headed towards the glowing eastern sky. The road to Sandy Flats was a flat for several miles before climbing up a ridge line and then oscillating up and down for a couple of miles before settling back down to the desert floor.

By the time they reached the flatter terrain on the other side of the ridge the sun was rising. A yellow orange glow glared at them and they shaded their eyes as best they could. Here the road largely stretched out in a long line across desolate sand. It was this terrain that lent itself to the name of Sandy Flats 25 miles northeast of where they were.

"Do you think something happened to them?" Beka asked leaning forward from the back seat.

Hastings shook his head. "I hope not." He glanced back and saw Beka's worried face. "I'm sure they're OK. Isn't this what they do all the time?"

Beka's eyes flicked over at Hastings and then back to the road ahead. "Yeah. I guess so."

"Well, there you go." Hastings said. "They know what they're doing. They know how to take care of themselves."

"Yeah." Beka said. There was a lack of enthusiasm in her voice.

Hastings frowned at her. "You seem to have a lack of faith in your team members."

Beka shook her head. "No. You're right. They've done this kind of thing many times before." Beka chose not to explain to Hastings that he was misinterpreting what she was feeling. She did have faith in Elliot and Robbie handling these kinds of situations. What bothered her was that her life had largely been that of a free spirit and this kind of situation, worrying about someone else, was something new to her.

It was unfamiliar territory and she didn't feel like she was prepared for how to deal with it.

"What's that?" Hasting asking pointing towards the road ahead.

Andrews shaded his eyes and stared. "Looks like a person."

"It's Robbie." Beka said.

They could see Regan standing in the road. He stood casually watching them as they drove up and stopped a few feet away.

Beka hopped out of the car and ran over to Regan. "I thought, well, that something might have happened to you." She stood close to him.

Regan shrugged. "Not too much. Just the usual. Giant monster spider attacked us and smashed the car."

Beka kissed Regan on the cheek. "Just the usual." She said with a smile.

"Where's the spider now?" Hastings asked.

Regan shook his head. "No idea. It's been hours since it was here."

Andrews spotted Simms down the short slope off the slide of the road next to the wreckage of their car. He walked down.

"You were in that?" Andrews asked Simms pointing at the car.

"Well," Simms said, "it was taller when we were in it. Most of the damage happened after we abandoned it."

The others walked down and joined Andrews and Simms.

"How did you not get eaten?" Hastings asked.

Simms waved over towards the culvert. "We ran into there."

"Did it try to get you in there?" Beka asked.

"It tried." Regan answered her.

"The power line is down about a mile further on." Simms said.

"So we know then that the monster is somewhere east of Desert Rock." Andrews said.

Simms nodded. "Yeah. Don't know what direction it went in. Too dark to track a black spider at night and no sign of it once it got light out."

Regan shook his head. "Doesn't make sense, though. The planes have covered this area pretty thoroughly by now. They should have spotted it by now."

"Agreed." Simms said. "There's something missing here." He was quiet for a moment. "I think we need some more information about this thing."

"You mean like someone that knows arachnids?" Hastings asked.

Simms shrugged slightly. "I don't know if a tarantula that has grown as big as this one will behave the same as the usual kind, but maybe just some general information on it's typical behavior might help."

"Well, as far as I know we don't have anyone in town with that kind of knowledge. I don't know that Steve could help with that. Her knowledge is focused more on the biochemical nature of living things than their behavior." Hastings said.

"It's alright. One of our other agents is a zoologist. He might be able to shed some light on why we can't seem to find this thing." Simms said. "Let's get back into town."

They all started back towards the car except Andrews he stood staring back down the road towards town.

Hastings looked back at the Sheriff. "Something wrong?"

Andrews shook his head. "No. I was just thinking that the farm where the wife went missing isn't far from here."

Beka thought for a moment. "Yeah. Now that you say that I seemed to remember seeing the spot where we turned off to go to his farm. It was back there a little way."

"That doesn't bode well for the missing wife." Simms said.

"No." Andrews said. "It doesn't."

They all climbed into the Sheriff's car and headed back into Desert Rock. They pulled up in front of the Sheriff's office just as Steve was emerging from it.

"I was looking for everyone. Didn't know where you'd gone." Steve said as they climbed out of the car.

"We were on a rescue mission." Beka said.

"You were a little late on the rescuing part." Regan said smiling at her.

"Did something happen?" Steve asked.

"I'll tell you all about it over some coffee." Hastings told Steve as he led her towards the restaurant.

"If you don't mind Sheriff, I have a couple of calls to make." Simms gestured towards the Sheriff's office.

"Sure." Andrews said. "But let me put in a call to the Power company first. I don't want any crews going out there to fix that line just yet."

"Of course." Simms said and the two of them went into the office.

"I was really worried." Beka said to Regan as they now stood alone on the sidewalk in front of the Sheriff's office.

"The tarantula fang piercing the roof of the car was a little disconcerting to me as well." Regan said.

"What?" Beka asked.

Regan waved it off. "Not important. I've told you. This is what we do."

"These monsters...I mean we read about them, but...I don't know...they're real." Beka said.

Regan nodded. "Yeah. They're real. It's why what we do is important. Find them. Identify them and, if possible, neutralize them."

"But every time you go after one of these things...I mean...anything could happen." Beka said.

"Yeah. It's kind of why the Director discourages us from having any kind of personal life. It...would be pretty hard on anyone waiting at home for us." Regan said.

They were both quiet for a moment.

"So...what does that mean?" Beka asked.

Regan looked at Beka. Based on company policy, he knew what he should say to her, but he didn't want to. In addition, he was never one to strictly adhere to company policies.

Regan sighed and put a hand on Beka's shoulder. "It means, if you're going to keep hanging around with me you're going to have to come to terms with that."

Beka thought for a moment. She was afraid Regan was going to tell her that it was time for her to go. She was relieved not to hear that. She smiled at Regan.

"OK, but no promises." Beka said.

Regan shrugged. "OK."

10

"Hey Elliot." Wyatt said. He was sitting on the edge of his desk at OSO headquarters in Washington D.C.

"Jonathon. I have a question for you." Simms said.

"OK. By the way, where are you guys? I thought you were due back from the West Coast days ago." Wyatt replied.

"We were redirected to Arizona to check something out." Simms said.

"Hmm. The Director didn't mention anything about that." Wyatt said.

"Not surprising. He is not much for small talk. Anyway, we have a bit of an issue here with a spider. A tarantula to be precise." Simms said.

"Oh? Well, tarantulas are fairly common out there in the desert. They're pretty harmless though." Wyatt said.

"Not when they get to be this size." Simms said.

"Oh. Yeah. I guess if you guys are out there it's probably not the garden variety of spider. So what's your question?" Wyatt asked.

"I was thinking as a zoologist you might be able to give us help in trying to track this thing down. We have been trying to spot it from the air, but, for some reason, the planes have found nothing. Doesn't make sense. This creature is easily 30 feet tall and at least 50 feet in diameter. Can't understand how the recon planes haven't spotted it." Simms said.

"Well, tarantulas are generally nocturnal so it's unlikely that it would be out during the daylight hours." Wyatt said.

"Ah. Good to know. The planes aren't flying at night and even if they were, it's doubtful they could spot a black spider in the dark." Simms said.

"Right." Wyatt agreed.

"So where does the tarantula go during the daytime?" Simms asked.

"Generally underground. It's cooler there and safer from predators." Wyatt said.

"Predators? What would what to go after a tarantula?" Simms asked.

"Birds, foxes, coyotes. Things like that." Wyatt said.

"Oh. Well, it's safe to say none of those are going after this spider." Simms said.

"Probably not." Wyatt agreed.

"Still, I don't think there are any caves around here. At least not ones large enough to accommodate something as big as this thing is." Simms said.

"Well a normal tarantula would find space under a rock or in a crevice somewhere. In lieu of that they can just dig into the sand and disappear for the day." Wyatt explained.

"Hmm." Simms thought for a moment. "I guess it's possible this creature might be able to dig itself into the sand."

"Yeah, I guess it could do that." Wyatt said.

"It would explain why the planes haven't been able to find it." Simms said.

"Yeah. I suppose you could tell the planes to look for areas where the sand has been disturbed." Wyatt suggested.

"Not sure about that. There seems to be a regular wind blowing around here. The sand is constantly in motion. Seems doubtful that the planes would be able to spot something like that." Simms said.

"Probably so." Wyatt said. "I'm not sure there's much alternative that to search the ground on foot."

Simms sighed. "Yeah. But it's a big desert out here."

"Right. You're going to need some help." Wyatt said.

"Agreed. I think I better call our friends at the nearest military base and get some boots out stomping around. OK. Thanks Jonathon. At least we have a plan now." Simms said.

"No problem." Wyatt said hanging up.

Simms walked into the restaurant. Sheriff Andrews, Hastings, Steve, Regan and Beka were all sitting at a table having coffee. Simms pulled up a chair and sat down.

"So what's the plan?" Regan asked.

"It seems our large friend is nocturnal. It hides in the daytime. Presumably by burying itself in the sand. So, the Air Force base has a contingent of soldiers stationed there. We're getting a couple of detachments to start combing the desert east of Desert Rock." Simms explained.

"If the spider is buried how are they going to find it?" Hastings asked. "They can't dig the whole desert up."

Simms smiled. "No. They can't dig up the whole desert, but they can riddle large sections of it with grenades and machine guns. That ought to stir the creature up."

"Yeah. I would think that would do it." Andrews agreed.

"And then what?" Steve asked.

"Then," Simms said, "the soldiers will attack it with bazookas and flamethrowers."

"Well, I guess now it is just a matter of waiting for them to find it." Hastings said. "Still, it's a lot of desert."

"Yeah." Regan said. "It's too bad there wasn't something to narrow down the search area even further. Something that gave a clue where the tarantula dug in at."

They sat around the table in silence for a minute.

Beka slapped the table and everyone except her jumped.

"Dust Devils!" Beka said.

"What?" Regan asked.

"Dust Devils." Beka repeated.

"You know those swirls of dust the wind stirs up." Andrews said. "Happens around here."

"Yeah. The farmer whose wife went missing. He said they were seeing more than usual." Beka said.

"You mean out by his ranch?" Hastings asked.

"Yeah." Beka nodded.

"You think these Dust Devil things out by the farmer's place are the tarantula digging in." Regan nodded. "That seems possible."

Andrews shrugged. "Yeah. I suppose it's possible."

"Where in relation to the farmer's place did these Dust Devils appear?" Simms asked.

"Uh, I don't know what direction, north or south, you know, that he pointed in." Beka said.

Andrews thought for a moment. "I know that place. Did he point towards the main road or away from it?"

Beka thought. "Kind of away, but not directly."

"Towards town or away from town?" Andrews asked.

Again Beka thought. "Away. Yes, away from town."

Andrews smiled. He looked at Simms. "Northeast."

Simms nodded. "Good work. You got a map?"

Andrews stood up. "In my office."

Simms got up and they headed out of the restaurant.

About two hours later several trucks rolled into the town of Desert Rock. The soldiers had started exiting the back of the trucks by the time Simms arrived and tracked down Major Johns, the commanding officer, a middle aged man with ruddy colored skin from the desert sun.

"So, you're the government guy I'm supposed to take orders from." Johns said shaking Simms' hand.

"I am and I need your soldiers to load back into the trucks." Simms said.

Major Johns' face turned to a scowl. "I was told we were being deployed here to protect the town folk from some...creature."

Simms shook his head. "No Major. You're here to hunt down the creature and destroy it."

The Major's face lit up. "Well, I'll be damned." Johns turned towards his men and called out. "Back in the trucks boys. We're going huntin' for a monster."

There was a general bit of cheering from the troops.

Johns turned back to Simms. "Generally we're just doin' guard duty at the base. Pretty boring. The boys'll be real happy to have something interestin' to do. You know, let off a little steam."

Simms nodded slightly. "OK. Well, this creature is about 30 feet tall and about 50 feet across. It has eight legs and huge fangs. This is not a day at the beach, Major."

Major Johns slapped Simms on the shoulder with a chuckle. "Don't you worry about my boys, Mr. Government guy. They'll be up for a good fight."

"You brought the bazookas and flamethrowers with you?" Simms asked.

Johns nodded. "Sure did. We're ready for anything."

"Let's hope so." Simms said. He pulled a map out of his pocket and opened it up. He pointed out where the soldiers needed to deploy. Simms had spent the last hour working through a plan how they might search for the tarantula and what to do once they found it. 15 minutes later the trucks were rolling out of Desert Rock and heading east.

Regan and Beka walked up to Simms as he stood in the street and watched the departing trucks.

"So they know where they're going what they're looking for?" Regan asked.

Simms nodded. "Yeah. I've split them up into three groups. We'll have two groups with grenades and machine guns sweeping through the area from the southwest to the northeast. The third group will have the heavy equipment. Once one of the other groups finds our friend we'll send in the bazookas and flamethrowers to kill it."

Regan nodded in agreement. "Sounds like a workable plan."

"Is this in the area of that farmer's place?" Beka asked.

"Near there. Yeah." Simms said.

"So, are we heading out there too?" Regan asked.

Simms hesitated. "I'm going out to make sure the deployment goes according to plan. I...would like you to call the Director."

"OK." Regan looked at Simms. Typically Simms was the one to talk to the Director. "You want me to give him an update on things?"

"You can, but he left a message earlier. I just think one of us should give him a call back. I think he was expecting us to be done with this business sooner than this." Simms said.

"Something going on?" Regan asked.

Simms shrugged. "Don't know. His message indicated he was concerned about something back in California."

"Not another sea monster I hope." Beka said.

Simms shook his head. "No. I don't think so. Anyway, I think it's something Wayne and Wyatt will need to deal with. We can't leave here until this creature is dead."

"OK. I will check in with the boss." Regan said. He and Beka turned headed back up the street towards the Sheriff's office while Simms climbed into the jeep the Army left for him and drove off east out of town.

11

"You're back." Regan said as Simms walked into the Sheriff's office. "I was about to round up a car and head out there."

Simms, holding a rolled up map, waved off Regan. "No need. Used up most of today getting the soldiers encamped in their respect search areas and explaining the general plan for how they will fan out and search in the morning. Also, went over what the plan was if they do find the creature."

Regan nodded. Andrews slid his feet off the desk and leaned forward.

"You think these guys can kill this monster from the ground?" Andrews asked.

Simms nodded. "I think so. The other tarantula was killed with napalm. These soldiers are more heavily armed than your people were and they have the flamethrowers if that is what it takes to kill it."

Simms turned to Regan. "What did the Director have to say?"

"Not much. He is concerned about something going on near some small town in Southern California. He didn't elaborate on what it was." Regan answered.

"OK. Well, we can't worry about that right now." Simms said.

"Is that the deployment of the soldiers?" Regan asked pointing at the maps.

"Yeah." Simms laid the map down on Andrews' desk and unrolled it. "We have a company deployed at this end of the sandy plain east of town. The other company is over here. They will stretch out between the higher ground north and south and work towards each other. The heavier weapons are stationed here, roughly half way between each group."

"So they won't start until morning?" Andrews asked.

"Yeah." Simms said. "I considered having them deploy at night with searchlights, but decided against it. I think that creature might be too hard to spot in the dark."

"Yeah, that might get a little risky." Regan agreed.

"Well, I guess there isn't anything more to do right now until the morning." Simms said.

"Right." Regan said.

The sun dropped below the distant horizon and, as is the case in the desert, the darkness quickly enveloped the desert surrounding the base camp of Company B. Private Walker sat on the tire of the small trailer that carried one of the dozen searchlights that the soldiers had brought with them. They had been ordered to deploy the lights in a semi-circle around their encampment. They had encamped up against a small rock face at the south side of the sandy valley they were in. Above them, a short distance further south, was the main road that led back into Desert Rock, several miles west.

"Where the hell's the generator?" Walker asked Private Downs.

Downs had just joined Walker at the light. He shrugged. "Don't know. They were having trouble getting it started."

"Well, how we supposed to see anything in the dark?" Walker asked, his Arkansas accent clearly on display.

Downs shrugged again. "Don't know."

Walker stared out at the blackness that was a massive stretch of sand just 20 minutes earlier. He wasn't too worried. There was some big spider out here that they were supposed to kill. Spiders didn't bother him. He was pretty sure no spider he'd ever seen could stand up to his M1 carbine.

In the distance behind Walker and Downs the sound of an engine coughing to life was heard. There was a loud whistle from somewhere near the generator which Walker knew was the signal to turn on the lights. He stood up and circled around the tire and flipped a large lever. The light shot out across the sand. They could see pretty well about 100 feet out from where they stood.

Walker stared out along the beam of light. Nothing. No big spider. He went back to sitting on the tire and rested his rifle across his lap. Downs stood a few feet away and lit up a cigarette.

"So, we just stand here for a few hours watching for a big bug?" Downs asked.

Walker shrugged. "Guess so. That's what the Sergeant said to do."

"Seems like a waste of time." Downs said. "I heard there's lots of big bugs out here. What's one more or less?"

Walker shook his head. "Don't know."

They were quiet for a few minutes.

"Did you hear something?" Downs said staring out at the sand and the darkness beyond.

"Like a thumping sound?" Walker asked.

"Yeah. Like a thumping sound." Downs nodded.

Walker stood up and both soldiers raised there rifles slightly. Moments passed and nothing seemed to be stirring out in the darkness. Walker finally sat back down.

"Nothing I guess." Walker said.

"Guess not." Downs agreed.

After another few minutes Downs sat down in the sand. Walker leaned against the light, being careful not to touch the metal immediately surrounding the light itself. He had done that one other time, at the base, and learned just how hot the housing for the light got.

An hour passed and the desert was so quiet that when the shouting and gun fire started it caught both soldiers off guard. They both jumped to their feet. The sounds were coming from across the encampment.

"What is it?" Downs asked excitedly.

"Don't know." Walker said, his voice edgy.

"Should we go see?" Downs asked.

Walker shook his head as the gun fire became more intense. "I don't think so. I think we're supposed to stay at our post."

Another minute passed and the gun fire died down. Sergeant Rosen came trotting along around the perimeter. He was saying something to each of the searchlight crews. He came to Downs and Walker.

"God damn it! Turn around. You're supposed to be watching the perimeter." Rosen yelled at them.

"But..." Downs pointed in the direction the sound of gun fire had come from.

"Never mind that. Something tried to breach the perimeter. It was big and it moved fast, but we drove it off. You just mind your sector, understood." Rosen pointed off into the desert.

"Yes sir." Both Walker and Downs replied. They turned and stared out into the night.

Rosen nodded and trotted off to the next sentry post.

The camp grew quiet again. An hour dragged by. Walker was back to sitting on the tire of the trailer and Downs had returned to sitting cross legged on the sand staring blankly out into the dark. Finally Downs stood up and brushed sand off his pants.

"I need to take a piss." Downs said.

Walker only sighed.

Downs walked around to the other side of the trailer and pissed on the wheel. He always thought it was funny, peeing on the equipment. He finished his business and glanced out into the distance of the light cast out by the searchlight. He stared. He tilted his head. Something looked funny out there.

"What the hell...?" Downs said.

"What?" Walker said, still sitting on the tire on the opposite side of the trailer.

"I don't know. Looks weird." Downs said.

Walker stood up and stretched. "What looks weird?"

"Out there." Downs pointed.

Walker looked out where Downs was pointing. It took him a moment to see what Downs was referring to. Something did look funny out there. The arc of the light lit up about a 30 degree wedge which grew wider the further out away from the light it went. About 50 or 60 feet out there was a section of the lighted arc that was not lit up. It was like something was shadowing that spot, but there was nothing in front of it. Just a band of unlit darkness in one part of the lighted area.

Downs took several steps forward tilting his head, as if that might help him discern what he was seeing. Walker took a step forward as well.

Suddenly the odd dark strip shifted to the right and an additional strip of blackness appeared a couple of yards to the left of the first one.

"What the hell is it?" Downs asked.

"I don't—-" Walker started.

Both black strips shifted again and this time another bigger thicker black strip appeared closer to them. Then another one appeared even closer, but they weren't shadows or black strips. They were more like black posts that someone was slamming into the sand in front of them.

Walker thought he saw something higher up blocking out the stars and he staggered backwards.

"What is..." Downs started asking.

Walker lifted his rifle and started firing in the general direction of where the stars were disappearing. That seemed to wake Downs up and he scrambled back to the trailer. He had to circle around it to snatch up his rifle. He knelt in the sand next to Walker and began firing into a vague blackness that seemed to be moving and shifting around in front of them.

They could sense rather than hear others running up behind them. More gun fire echoed out into the night air, but the black shape did not move away. It seemed to be affected by the gun fire, but only to the extent that it continued to shift around in the beam of light. It seemed like the bullets merely stung it, but did no real damage.

Suddenly someone was standing right next to Walker. With a roar the area in front of them lit up from the spewing flame of a flamethrower. For a brief instant the men got a clear view of a massive black body, giant black orbs, its eyes, and even a glimpse of two large fangs. Then the flames blocked the view and equally fast the black monster bounded away and was gone.

The flame disappeared as did the gun fire. It was quiet. Everyone simply stood there staring out into the beam of light and the blackness beyond. Finally a series of curses and mumbled comments circulated through the men.

"Alright." Rosen said, suddenly standing in the midst of the men. "We're doubling up at every post. And we're going to keep those flamethrowers handy."

"Jesus." Downs said.

"You said it." Walker said. "That was one big ass spider."

"Yeah." Downs said standing slowly up. "And I think I need to take another piss."

12

"So they're deploying right now?" Simms asked the jeep driver.

"Yes sir." The driver said hanging the mic of the radio back up.

Simms glanced back at Regan and Beka. They were still standing back along the street in front of the Sheriff's office. He turned and stared out at the rising sun in the East. He turned at the sound of someone walking up behind him.

"Good morning, Doctor." Simms said.

"Good morning." Hastings replied. He was silent for a moment, but it was clear something was on his mind.

"You're about to go out to where the soldiers are?" Hastings asked.

Simms nodded. "I am."

"Um, so, I wanted to ask you a question. I mean, if its not, you know, confidential or anything." Hastings said hesitantly.

Simms looked at Hastings. "OK..."

"Well, what I was wondering is this. Why is the government interested in Deemer's work?" Hastings asked.

Simms studied Hastings for a moment. "I...am not aware that the government is interested in Professor Deemer's work."

Hastings hesitated. "I thought you had indicated the government was interested in getting a hold of Deemer's work."

"Oh. That. OK, yes, the OSO would be interested in looking over Professor Deemer's work, but not to confiscate it. You see, back in the 30s the OSO was involved in trying to stop an individual by the name Zeitner. He had been doing work along similar lines of Professor Deemer's work. He had been even more successful than Deemer. It...led to some serious danger for, well, everyone. Anyway, when Zeitner was finally stopped the OSO was unable to account for where his research went. It was lost. Ever since then there has been a constant concern that work was disseminated to other, equally less scrupulous individuals." Simms explained.

"And you think Deemer's work may be derived from this Zeitner's work?" Hastings asked.

Simms shrugged. "Possibly. We would like to at least examine his notes to see if there is sufficient similarity with Zeitner's work to conclude that it is in fact based on it. It would give us a potential lead on finding Zeitner's original work. Keeping Zeitner's work out of the hands of those that would exploit it for profit or political gain could potentially save a great many lives."

Hastings nodded solemnly. "I understand."

"Do you have any ideas on where Professor Deemer's notes ended up?" Simms asked.

Hastings shook his head. "Not offhand, but I will surely let you know if I do." Hastings moved off before Simms could reply.

Regan and Beka walked up to Simms.

"Are we headed out to the staging area where the big weapons are?" Regan asked.

Simms nodded. "Yeah. We'll wait for the soldiers to turn up something."

"So...by we, who does that all entail?" Beka asked.

Simms hesitated. He almost reflexively told her she was staying behind. But, the truth was, she hadn't been a burden to them. In addition, he had to admit, that having and extra person available was helpful sometimes.

Simms sighed. It did, though, go against some long standing rule that had, somewhere along the way, been drilled into him.

"I am going to climb into the front seat of this jeep." Simms said. "And I am not going to look at who might be getting in the back."

Beka smiled at Simms. She knew it was a victory, but she didn't feel victorious. She felt, for the first time in a long time, like she had a place somewhere in this world.

"Does that mean I can stay behind?" Regan asked with a smirk. Beka slapped Regan in the shoulder.

Simms gave Regan a look and climbed into the jeep. Beka, carrying what looked like a large purse, and Regan climbed into the back of the jeep. The driver started the jeep and they drove off to the East and into the early morning sun.

They drove until they reached where the road climbed up into the hills. At the top of a rise they found a couple of military trucks. The soldiers were milling about, talking and checking some of the equipment. The jeep pulled off the road behind a truck.

Simms checked with the captain in charge of these men and went over the plan for the second time this morning. At Regan's request the jeep driver went around and found a couple pairs of binoculars.

The view from the side of the road stretched out across a large sandy plain to the north. Regan scanned the distant sands and he thought he could just make out, to the west, the traces of some small dots moving slowly along. That would be soldiers working their way across the valley. There was also the faint sounds of something. Regan knew that it was the sound of gun fire as the soldiers were shooting into the sand ahead of them in an effort to flush out the creature.

Simms joined Beka and Regan at the edge of the sloping hillside. Beka handed Simms the other set of binoculars and Regan pointed in the direction he had seen the soldiers. Simms stared at them for a minute or two.

"Well, I guess we just wait now." Simms said, turning towards a cluster of rocks and sitting down. Regan and Beka joined him.

The morning slowly dragged along. Occasionally Regan or Simms got up and scanned the distant valley of sand, but nothing other than the steady movement of the soldiers seemed to be happening.

"So, how did that thing not kill thousands of Japanese?" Beka asked.

"It did." Regan said. "You can't just waltz through a city like Tokyo knocking down buildings and not kill lots of people."

"I remember it being on the news, but they didn't say anything about lots of people being killed." Beka said.

"The Japanese government wanted to limit that information. They felt it would look like their military strength was weak and depleted. They felt that they would appear vulnerable." Simms said.

"Wow." Beka said, dabbing some sweat off her forehead as the sun climbed into the midday sky. "Is anyone hungry?"

Simms and Regan looked at each other and then at Beka.

Beka's eyes narrowed. "You guys didn't bring any food, did you?"

"Well...there might be some rations in the trucks somewhere..." Simms said slowly.

Beka shook her head. "I don't know how men can fight wars when they are so awful at planning." She stood up and walked to the jeep. She pulled out her over sized purse and returned to where they were sitting. Setting the bag down she pulled out several wrapped sandwiches and a thermos with water in it.

"You brought a picnic?" Simms asked.

"I thought that was just a big purse." Regan said.

Beka looked at Regan. "What would I need a big purse out here for?"

Regan started to point at his face and then his hair. He stopped. Beka's look told him he was being an idiot.

"Right. Sandwiches. Good idea." Regan said taking a sandwich from Beka.

Simms quietly took a sandwich. He couldn't decide if he was disturbed about having a little picnic while on a mission or embarrassed that he didn't think about supplies. They ate in silence.

The first indication of something came subtly. Simms was in the process of taking another bite of his sandwich when he stopped with the sandwich hovering just in front of his mouth.

"You've got to put it all the way up to your mouth to take a bite." Beka said looking at Simms.

Simms turned his head towards the Army trucks by the road. He sat motionless for a moment. Regan was about to say something when the sound drew his attention as well. It was the indistinguishable, yet clearly excited chatter of voices coming over the trucks' radios.

Simms tossed his sandwich away and hustled over to the nearest truck. Regan followed.

"What? Am I missing something?" Beka said calling after them. After cleaning up the makeshift picnic Beka walked over to where they were standing next to the truck.

"What is it? Beka asked.

Simms just shook off her question.

"Don't know." Regan answered her. "Too much cross talk. Can't tell what's going on."

Simms quickly turned and walked around the front of the truck. "Captain!"

A soldier came running over.

"Get on the radio and clear all that chatter and find out what's going on." Simms said. He waved back towards the truck.

"Yes sir." The captain said and scrambled up into the truck.

"Hey, I think I hear something." Regan said and started walking back towards the spot they had been eating at. Simms and Beka followed. When they reached the spot they could faintly hear sounds from somewhere in the distance. Through binoculars they could see puffs of dust obscuring what was going on. Even with the dust though both Regan and Simms could see something large and black moving.

"There it is!" Simms said. He spun around and headed back towards the trucks. Regan handed his binoculars to Beka.

"Is that it?" Beka asked staring through the binoculars.

"Yeah. That's it." Regan said.

"I thought it would be bigger." Beka commented.

"You're about twenty miles away." Regan said. "It looks a hell of a lot bigger when you're standing right in front of it and its trying to eat you."

"I...think I'm close enough right here." Beka said.

Behind them they could here the voices of soldiers and the sound of men climbing up into the trucks. Regan turned and looked back over at Simms. He was waving for Regan to join them.

"I have to go." Regan said looking at Beka.

Beka hesitated. Generally she liked being in on the action, but a giant spider...she couldn't stand the little ones. "I guess...you would prefer I stay here."

"I would." Regan said.

"OK." Beka said.

"Really?" Regan asked, surprised at Beka's quick agreement.

"Well, I'm a team player. I follow orders." Beka said.

"Since when?" Regan asked.

"Since I hate spiders." Beka answered.

"Right." Regan nodded. "Well, why don't you take the jeep back into town and let them all know we found the creature."

Beka saluted. "Sure thing, boss."

Regan trotted over to Simms and a moment later Simms yelled instructions to the jeep driver. Then Simms and Regan climbed up into the back of one of the trucks and all the vehicles sped away.

13

All three trucks stopped just short of the dry river bed. The sandy ground dropped several feet straight down into a long flat bed of sand that meandered in both directions as far as one could see. When there was rain in the distant hills water would come rushing through here, but there was little if any rain this time of year. Still, for the trucks, the twenty foot wide dry river bed blocked their way.

The soldiers, along with Simms and Regan, climbed out of the trucks and stood at the edge of the empty river bed. They had a very clear view of the Spider and the soldiers trying to hold it back from this spot, less than a mile away.

"Guess we walk from here." Regan said.

"Guess so." Simms said.

They could here the captain getting his men prepared. They pulled on flamethrowers and organized the bazookas with their ammo. As soon as they were ready the men began sliding down the embankment. Crossing the sandy river bed they scrambled up the other side and began moving as fast as they could towards the large black enemy.

In the distance were a couple of screams as the creature hopped forward and into the skirmish line the soldiers had established in front of it. Their job was to keep the spider engaged and occupied until the flamethrowers and bazookas arrived. It was a dangerous task since the bullets seemed to do little damage to the spider. Essentially their skirmish line was a slow and steady retreat.

"So...what exactly is our task here?" Regan asked. He held up his .45 pistol when Simms looked over at him.

Simms glanced down at his own .45 and then at Regan. "Our task is to make sure this thing is killed. As far as these are concerned..." Simms waved his gun, "I guess I just feel better holding some kind of gun rather than nothing."

Regan shrugged as they jogged towards the Spider. "I suppose."

The captain in charge of the soldiers forming the skirmish saw the line of flamethrowers drawing near and called out to his men. Almost in unison the soldiers broke into a run fleeing back towards the line of heavier weapons coming to their assistance. While the captain's intention was to spare any more of his men from being killed by the spider by getting them as quickly as possible out of harm's way it was, in fact, a bad decision. He was a captain in the Army—-not a biologist.

When the spider saw the men begin running its natural predator instinct kicked in. It quickly began chasing men down and killing them in short order. The creature wasn't even eating the men, just killing them.

Simms watched what was happening and veered to his right. Grabbed the shoulder of a soldier carrying a bazooka. The soldier spun slightly towards Simms with a surprised expression.

"Can you hit that thing from here?" Simms yelled at the soldier.

The soldier glanced at the spider then back at Simms. "I...I don't know."

"You need to try." Simms said.

"But...if I'm short I could kill one of our guys." The soldier said.

Simms pointed at the carnage the spider was now wreaking upon the fleeing men. "They're being slaughtered now. Try."

The soldiers knelt down. He set down a bag containing a few bazooka rounds and shouldered his bazooka. Simms fished out a round and slid it into the back of the bazooka. Simms tapped the helmet of the soldier and then looked up to see Regan still jogging forward and into the line of fire of the bazooka. While it was true the soldier had elevated the bazooka to maximize the distance he could reach with it, still, it was, in fact, against regulations to stand in front of someone firing a bazooka.

"Robbie!" Simms yelled.

Regan glanced back. He saw the bazooka and, realizing what was happening, dropped into the sand immediately in front of him. He hit the ground as he heard the whoosh of the bazooka.

The shell of the bazooka did fall short of the spider by several yards, but, fortunately, there were no soldiers there. The explosion shot a geyser of sand into the air. The blast of sand caught the spider's attention and it hesitated, staring at the spot where the sand still hung in the air.

Simms loaded up another shell into the bazooka. The second shot landed right next to the leg of the spider. The blast did not appear to harm the spider, but the creature clearly flinched. A second man carrying a bazooka had now stopped and another soldier loaded him up. His shot hit into the sand just under the front of the spider. This time the spider was knocked slightly off balance and then stood completely still, clearly unsure of what was happening.

A thought struck Simms as he watched the spider. He said something to the soldier with the bazooka in front of him. The soldier glanced up at Simms and lowered his bazooka. Simms ran over to the soldier firing the second bazooka and yelled something to him. A third soldier was prepping his bazooka as Simms waved him to stop.

It had occurred to Simms that the flamethrowers were still out of range to fire at the spider and if the spider decided to turn and run they would never catch up to it. Simms pointed at several of the soldiers with flamethrowers and waved them forward.

Since the spider had stopped moving forward the retreating soldiers were able to put a little distance between them and the black creature that towered over them. Fortunately, as the soldiers with the flamethrowers closed in the spider continued to stand still, totally motionless. It appeared to be baffled by what was happening before it.

Now, within range of the spider, Simms halted the soldiers with the flamethrowers and spread them out in a semi-circle around the front of the monster. Behind them several other soldiers with flamethrowers were catching up and the captain had rallied the soldiers with bazookas to form a line behind the flamethrowers.

Simms gave the signal and the soldiers began torching the giant spider. The moment the flames hit the spider it hopped backwards, but not clear of the spouting fire. The creature scrambled back some more getting just out of range of the flame throwers, but several legs and part of it's main body were already burning. It began turning to run.

The captain moved the bazooka line forward and they began firing at the creature. Most shots hit the sand around the spider, but two shots hit separate legs of the spider shattering them. One found the main body and a gaping hole appeared on the spider's side. Some kind of fluid began running out of the wound. The spider staggered. It's movements became slow and erratic. Another shot took out another leg and one more struck the main body leaving another hole not far from the first one. Moments later the monster slumped to the ground.

Simms ordered the soldiers carrying flamethrowers forward and they began systematically incinerating the creature.

"That's a big barbecue." Regan said as walked up to where Simms stood watching the flames.

"It stinks too." Simms said.

"I don't think we've ever come across a monster that didn't stink. Dead or alive." Regan said.

"True. Sad, but true." Simms agreed.

14

"Can I talk to you for a moment?" Hastings had just walked up to Simms.

Simms turned to look at Hastings. He had been standing on the street corner watching the trucks loaded up with soldiers driving through town. He was waiting for a report from one of the captains, the last one on the scene of the creature's destruction.

"Sure." Simms said. He noticed a soft leather briefcase under Hastings' arm.

Hastings eased the briefcase from under his arm and extended out to Simms. "I...thought you should have this."

Simms slowly took the briefcase. "Deemer's notes?"

"Yeah." Hastings nodded.

"Did you have them?" Simms asked.

Hastings was slow to answer. "No. If I did I would handed them over to you when you told me why the government wanted them."

"Dr. Clayton?" Simms asked.

"Yeah." Hastings answered. There was a bit of a haunted look in his eyes.

"Well," Simms said, "your government thanks you and I personally appreciate this. This could be very important."

Hastings nodded. "I understand." Hastings' eyes seemed to lock on to something behind Simms.

Simms turned to see Steve heading down the street straight towards them. She didn't look happy.

"Excuse me." Hastings said in a hoarse voice. He walked up the street to meet Steve.

Steve stopped as Hastings walked up to her. She stared cold and hard at Hastings.

"Why?" Steve asked after a moment.

Hastings sighed. "Because there are bigger things at stake here."

"Bigger than unlocking the secrets of life itself?" Steve asked incredulously.

"I don't know about the extent of what Deemer's work could lead to, but saving people's lives is more important than unlocking any secrets." Hastings said.

"This could have saved lots of people's lives." Steve replied.

Hastings shrugged. "I don't know. Maybe. Or maybe it could lead to more accidents like this mess." Hastings waved back in the general direction of the desert.

"I can't believe you would betray me like this." Steve said indignantly.

"I'm sorry, but I'm just a country doctor and keeping people safe is all I know. Something on this magnitude...its better in the hands of these OSO guys." Hastings said.

Steve stared at Hastings. Finally she spoke in a very tight voice. "You are just a country doctor. That's for damn sure." She turned and stiffly walked away.

Hastings stood and watched her go.

"What's that?" Regan asked as he and Beka joined Simms at a table in the restaurant.

Simms looked up from some papers he was shuffling around on the table in front of him.

"Deemer's notes." Simms said.

"You found them?" Regan asked.

"They found me." Simms said. "Hastings gave them to me. Dr. Clayton had them hidden away."

"Why was she hiding them?" Beka asked.

"Because I think she had plans to continue Deemer's work." Simms said.

"Ugh. We don't need any more accidents like this happening out there." Regan said.

"Agreed. But, more importantly, we need to see if there is anything here that might be related in some way to Zeitner's work." Simms said.

"True." Regan said.

"Zeitner?" Beka asked.

"Long story." Regan answered her. "I'll tell you about it some time."

The waiter appeared at their table. He seemed a little hesitant. Finally, he spoke up.

"You are those government people, right?" The waiter asked.

"That's right we're G-Men." Beka said.

The waiter, Simms and Regan looked at Beka.

"Well, G-People. Anyway..." Beka said trialing off.

"We are from the government, yes." Simms said.

"And you killed those giant spiders?" The waiter asked.

"We assisted in their destruction." Simms said nodding.

"So, what about the rabbit?" The waiter asked.

"Rabbit?" Regan asked.

The waiter looked at them. "Haven't you heard? Some folks say they have seen a giant white rabbit west of town."

Simms and Regan looked at each other. Simms shuffled a few papers and glanced at them.

"Damn." Simms said.

"What?" Beka asked.

Simms sighed. "Deemer used some rabbits in his experiments."

An awkward silence hung in the air.

"You know..." Regan said. "Rabbits are herbivores. Probably not much of a threat to people regardless of their size."

"And its only a rumor anyway." Beka pointed out.

Simms hesitated. He shook his head. He looked up at the waiter. "I'm going to pretend I didn't hear you and order some dinner."

"Me too." Regan said.

"I am starving." Beka added.

The waiter stared at them strangely and then took out his pad of paper. He took their order and left shaking his head.

"So, what's next?" Beka asked.

"We are headed back to Washington." Simms said.

There was a moment of silence.

"Are there going to be two tickets or three?" Beka asked quietly.

Simms looked over at Beka. "I think the OSO can afford three tickets."

Beka smiled. Regan smiled. Simms just shrugged.

Outside the window of the restaurant the last bus of the day pulled up to the curb. Simms, Regan and Beka looked out at it. Standing alone at the bus stop was Steve with her suitcase in hand. The doors of the bus opened and Steve, without a glance back, climbed on to the bus. A moment later the bus pulled away.

K McConnell

From the case files of the
Office of Scientific Operations:

Declassified File

Public Release #5B

File #171

1956

Commonly referred to by the public as
"Invasion of the Body Snatchers"

1

1956

Marcus Edmonds, the Director of the OSO, sat at the head of the conference table and glanced down at the piece of paper in front of him. He was not a tall man and the large chair at the head of the table made him seem even shorter. His silver hair stood out against the black leather of the chair's back. He appeared to be unsure about this meeting.

OSO Agent Thomas Wayne and Agent Jonathon Wyatt were also seated at the table. Jessica, Marcus' secretary sat in a chair near Marcus.

"As I said, I'm not sure there is anything to this or not." Marcus said.

"So, how long has Major McMaster been missing, again?" Wayne asked.

Marcus gestured towards Jessica. She glanced down at her notes.

"Three days." Jessica said.

"Doesn't seem that long for the Air Force to be missing someone." Wyatt said as he stared around at the sparse decor of the conference room. There was a framed document that was the original charter, signed by Franklin Roosevelt, on one wall and a framed photo of the current President, Eisenhower, on the opposite wall.

"I agree. I think there's more to this than they are telling us." Marcus nodded.

"So, you said that Major McMaster was investigating a meteor shower near the town of Santa Mira California and had reported something strange." Wayne said.

"And dangerous." Wyatt added.

Wayne glanced at Wyatt and nodded slightly shaking his black hair. "And, well, vaguely dangerous. Why isn't the Air Force just sending out their own people to find their missing Major?"

"It seems there was some kind of briefing at the White House and the President ordered the Air Force to enlist our help." Marcus answered.

"So what is our mission? Find this Major McMaster and bring him back to Washington?" Wyatt asked.

"Well, it was not made clear to me that we were to bring him back here. Just make contact with him and determine what exactly his cryptic reference to some kind of danger is." Marcus said.

"Can you read that message again?" Wyatt asked.

Again Marcus gestured to Jessica.

Jessica lifted up a piece of paper and read from it. "People are not right. Origin unclear. Extent of danger unknown." Jessica set the paper back down.

"People are not right. What is that supposed to mean?" Wyatt asked. He pushed a hand through his sandy brown hair. "Hell, people are wrong all the time about all kinds of things. That's hardly a national crisis."

"Maybe he means there is something wrong with the people." Wayne said.

"Have we heard of any reports from out there of any kind of trouble? Or anything out of the ordinary?" Wyatt asked looking at Marcus.

Marcus turned to Jessica. "Have Riley come in here, please."

Jessica got up and left the room.

Marcus looked back to Wyatt. "I have not gotten any reports of trouble or anything odd from anywhere near this Santa Mira. I did ask Riley to put a call through to the sheriff of Santa Mira to see if they were having any problems."

The door to the conference room opened and Jessica returned to her seat. The young lieutenant, Riley who served the OSO as their primary communications officer stood in the door way.

"Any luck on our call?" Marcus asked Riley.

Riley nodded. "Yes sir. I just got through a few minutes ago. I ran through my script and he was surprised that the Department of the Interior would be checking with him about any earthquake tremors or any other anomalies, but told me that everything in Santa Mira was just fine. Nothing out of the ordinary."

"Thank you." Marcus said with a nod that told Riley he was excused.

"So, it seems to me," Wayne said thoughtfully, "that it comes down to one of three possibilities. First, there is nothing odd going on in Santa Mira and that our lost Air Force Major was suffering from a little heat stroke inspired paranoia. Or, second, that the Major did find something strange is going on in Santa Mira, but the authorities in Santa Mira are currently unaware of what's going on. And, finally, that something nefarious is happening out there and the authorities are a part of it."

"Nefarious?" Wyatt asked. "How did you decide on nefarious?"

"Nefarious. Like something bad happening." Wayne said.

"Yeah, I know what nefarious is, but it implies bad intention. Most of the monsters we encounter do not have evil plans. I don't think we can jump to nefarious at this point." Wyatt said.

"I think nefarious is a perfectly reasonable assumption if there is some kind of danger being perpetrated in the city of Santa Mira and the authorities are covering it up." Wayne replied.

"Gentlemen," Marcus said, "we will not, for the moment, decide if there is a nefarious nature to the situation in Santa Mira. It will be your task to make contact with Major McMaster and evaluate the extent of the danger, if any, to the citizens of Santa Mira and the surrounding area."

"Right." Wayne said.

"Got it." Wyatt agreed.

"On your way." Marcus said with a wave of his hand.

Wayne and Wyatt got up and walked out of the conference room.

"What about sinister?" Wayne asked as the two of them collected items, including their OSO issued .45s, from their respective desks.

Wyatt slowly shook his head. "Nope. Not really sold on that word at the moment either."

Wayne sighed. "Some people are just hard to please."

2

The bus pulled up to the curb in the center of Santa Mira and stopped. Wayne and Wyatt had flown into Sacramento and taken a bus to Santa Mira. It was the last bus of the day and the evening sun was dropping down over the distant ridges.

The few people on the bus were slow to get off. Wayne and Wyatt were the last ones to step down from the bus and into the quiet street. Immediately as they stepped out a man walked up to them.

"Excuse me gentlemen, but the police chief has asked all newly arrived people to accompany me to the school gymnasium. If you would be so kind as to follow me." The man, somewhere in his forties wearing a casual suit, a hat and a strange, seemingly forced smile, made a gesture in a particular direction.

Wayne glanced at Wyatt and then back at the man. Neither of them moved. Wayne reached into his jacket and pulled out his wallet. He opened it up and showed it the man.

"We are from the Office of Scientific Operations. We would be interested in talking to your police chief directly." Wayne said.

The man glanced at Wayne's ID. His expression indicated he had no idea what he was looking at. He hesitated.

"If you could just follow me, I'm sure everything can be settled at the school." The man said as he made another gesture towards a destination further up the street. This time he took a step in that direction watching Wayne and Wyatt, but they still didn't move.

"Where is the police chief?" Wyatt asked the man.

Again the man hesitated. It was apparent that other people that he had asked to do this had complied without any further prompting.

"The...police chief wants everyone to go to the school gymnasium." The man said, as if that was explanation enough.

"Why?" Wyatt asked.

The man stared at them blankly.

"Because the police chief said so." The man said flatly.

"Is the police chief at the school right now?" Wayne asked.

Again the man's expression was blank. "I...don't know."

Wayne looked at Wyatt. "I don't know if we need to find him initially anyway."

"Agreed." Wyatt said.

Wayne looked back at the man. "We'll tour your school another time—-maybe."

Wayne and Wyatt started walking across the street towards the sidewalk and a building further up the street, the opposite direction the man was trying to direct them, towards a sign indicating a hotel.

"But...the school...?" The man stammered.

"Give our regards to the school." Wyatt said over his shoulder.

They walked into the hotel. The lobby was empty and quiet. A man stood behind the front desk. He looked up was Wayne and Wyatt walked in each carrying a small travel bag. The man behind the desk looked surprised and puzzled.

"We'd like a room." Wayne said.

The man hesitated. "Did you just get off the bus?"

Wayne nodded. "We did."

"You're...supposed to go to the school—-" The man started to say.

"Gymnasium." Wayne finished his sentence. "Yes, we heard that already."

"Must be one hell of an interesting gymnasium." Wyatt said.

"But..." The man stammered.

"The room." Wayne said. "This is a hotel, isn't it?"

"If it's not," Wyatt said waving back towards the front door, "then your sign's messed up."

"Uh, yes, but..." The man looked past Wayne and Wyatt at the front door as if he was expecting someone else to come through it and clarify something.

"The room. Or are we going to have to just sleep here in the lobby?" Wayne asked.

"Uh, OK." He slowly turned around and pulled a key off the board behind him full of keys hanging on hooks. "Room 209." He produced a book from under the counter, flipped it open and slid it across to Wayne.

Wayne signed both of their names into the ledger and accepted the key.

"Up the stairs," the man spoke slowly and gestured towards a set of stairs directly across the small lobby, "to the right and straight."

"Thank you." Wayne said.

"Are you familiar with an Air Force officer by the name of McMaster?" Wyatt asked.

The man stared straight at Wyatt without any expression. "No sir. Never heard of anyone by that name."

Wayne and Wyatt exchanged a glance and headed up the stairs. The room was at the front of the building. There were two twin beds and they dropped their bags on to the beds. Wayne walked to the small window that looked down on to the square in the middle of town where the bus had dropped them off.

"We seem to be of some interest to these people." Wayne said letting the dusty curtain drop back across the window.

"Really." Wyatt said scanning the room.

"There are three people out in the street staring up at this window and one of them is our friendly hotel clerk." Wayne said.

"Well, what's the plan?" Wyatt asked.

"I am thinking maybe we should have a look at the site McMaster said the meteors landed at." Wayne said.

Wyatt nodded. "Sounds good. Of course we will need a car for that."

Wayne pointed back at the window. "I saw a used car lot just up the street. We'll just buy one."

Wyatt looked dubiously at Wayne. "How is that going to slide through Accounting?"

Wayne shrugged. "We'll sell it back when we're done."

"You know it never works that way. The moment we buy that at OSO expense that sucker's doomed to be blown up or crushed by some giant creature at some point." Wyatt said shaking his head.

"I would like to disagree with that, but, well, past experience...." Wayne said.

"Right." Wyatt nodded as they walked out the door.

They exited the hotel and started walking up the street while several people at various points along the street seemed to be watching them.

"Am I paranoid in thinking that all these people are watching us or...are they all actually watching us because *they* are paranoid?" Wyatt asked glancing about.

"I don't know, but something odd is definitely going on here." Wayne said.

They strolled on to the used car parking lot. A man watched them from the window of a small office. He came out of the office and hesitantly walked towards them.

"Can I help you?" The man was short with a small thin black mustache and black hair swooped to one side of his head. His tone of voice was flat and he did not seem genuinely interested in helping them.

"We would like to buy a car." Wayne said.

The man hesitated. "Why?"

"What do you mean, why?" Wyatt asked. "We want to buy a car so we can drive it."

"Drive where?" The man asked. He stared straight at them without any expression.

"Wherever we choose to." Wayne said slowly.

"Are you going to sell us a car or not?" Wyatt asked.

Again the man hesitated. "Yeah. Sure. Any one you want." The man made a vague wave towards the cars on the lot. He didn't seem to be inclined to assist them in choosing. He continued to stand staring at them.

Wayne and Wyatt looked at each other and then slowly scanned the lot.

"How about that one?" Wayne pointed at '49 Studebaker, a four door sedan.

The man shrugged. He turned and pulled the cardboard sign out of the window and Wayne paid him. The man retreated to the small office and returned with the keys. Wayne signed a slip of paper. Moments later Wayne and Wyatt were pulling out of the lot.

They drove south along the main street through town. They weren't exactly sure where they were headed, but they knew that somewhere southwest of the city of Santa Mira is where the meteors had landed. After a couple of wrong turns they finally ended up on Jackson Drive which was a two lane that seemed to head straight southwest out of the city.

The sun was working its way down the sky towards the low ridges to the west, but there was still plenty of daylight for them to be able to track down the location of the meteors.

They were only about 2 miles out of the city when something appeared to be blocking the road ahead of them. As they drew closer it turned out to be two delivery trucks parked across the road, blocking traffic in either direction. Two men stood next to the trucks.

Wayne brought the car to a stop a few feet in front of the trucks. One of the two men, a burly dark haired man walked up to the side of the car.

"Is there a problem?" Wayne asked.

The burly man looked them over before speaking. "Power lines are down. Can't get through."

"What happened to them?" Wyatt asked scanning the power lines running alongside the road.

The burly man was slow to answer. "The lines are down."

"Yeah." Wyatt said. "You mentioned that already."

"Can't get through." The burly man said flatly.

"You covered that part already too." Wyatt said.

"There were some meteors that came down in this vicinity. Know anything about that?" Wayne asked the man.

The second man, a smaller and slender blonde haired man with sun aged skin, walked up to Wyatt's side of the car.

"We don't anything about meteors. The power lines are down. No one can go through here." The second man said.

Wayne and Wyatt exchanged a look. It was a question about whether to use their authority to push on past these guys or not. Both Wayne and Wyatt seemed to recognize that the situation could end up becoming serious if they persisted.

Wayne slipped the car into reverse and back away from the two men. He turned the car around and they headed back into town.

"Maybe we should have a talk with this police chief." Wayne said.

"Hopefully he will be a little less wooden than the rest of these people are." Wyatt said.

"That wouldn't take much." Wayne said with a nod.

They drove back down along the main street of the town until they spotted the police station. Wayne parked the car at the curb and they walked into the police station. Two men were sitting in the small office. One was behind a desk and was clearly the police chief.

The police chief's eyes narrowed when they walked in. He scanned them carefully.

"I don't think I remember seeing the two of you at the school." Police Chief Nick Grivett said standing up.

"Yeah. Guess we missed the party." Wyatt said.

"I don't think I find your attitude very amusing." Grivett said, but his tone lacked any emotion.

"Well, it really wasn't meant to be all that amusing." Wyatt said.

Wayne pulled out his ID and held it out towards Grivett. "We are agents Wayne and Wyatt from the OSO—-the Office of Scientific Operations. We are here on official business."

Wyatt waved his ID in Grivett's direction.

Grivett stared at them for moment. "The what?"

"The Office of Scientific—-we're with the government." Wyatt said.

Grivett still stared at them suspiciously. Finally, he said, "What can I help you with?"

Wayne tucked his ID away. "We are looking for an Air Force officer by the name of Major McMaster."

Grivett shook his head. "Never heard of him."

"You're sure?" Wyatt asked.

Grivett stared hard at Wyatt. "I know everyone in this town and there's no one like that here. If he was here then he's left and gone somewhere else."

Wayne glanced at the other police officer still sitting in a chair. He sat blankly watching the scene without saying anything.

"If you know everyone in this town then you must recognize someone not from around here." Wyatt said.

"Yes." Grivett said with a slight shrug.

"And you haven't seen any strangers in your town recently?" Wyatt asked.

"I am looking at two right now." Grivett said.

Wyatt was about to say something when Wayne lightly grabbed his shirt sleeve. "Well, we'll leave you to your work. We appreciate your time."

With a glance back at Grivett, Wyatt followed Wayne out the door.

"He's not telling us something." Wyatt said when they were outside.

"I know." Wayne said. "Just like everyone else here. I don't think we're going to get any help or cooperation from anybody in Santa Mira."

"You think they are all in on some big secret conspiracy here?" Wyatt asked as they climbed back into the car.

"Maybe. Sure seems like it is something like that." Wayne answered.

They drove back to the hotel and parked in the small lot next to the building. Walking into the lobby of the hotel they saw the hotel clerk watching them.

Wyatt stopped halfway across the lobby. Wayne stopped to look back at Wyatt from the foot of the stairs.

Wyatt turned towards the hotel clerk. He waved at the brightly lit hotel. "Guess the power lines south of town aren't affecting anything in Santa Mira."

The hotel clerk stared at Wyatt. "Power lines?"

"Yeah, the road's blocked I guess because of some power lines being down." Wyatt said watching the clerk.

The hotel clerk stared blankly at Wyatt for a moment before speaking. "Yes. Yes, the power lines are down. We get our power from somewhere else."

"Right." Wyatt said and walked to the stairs.

3

"Well, this is a nice quiet dinner." Wyatt said as they sat in a restaurant just down the street from their hotel.

Wayne nodded slowly while very covertly glancing around at the rest if the restaurant's patrons. There were only a few people in the restaurant and they were eating in almost total silence.

"Usually, I would appreciate a calm environment to enjoy my dinner in, but this..." Wayne said.

Wyatt nodded his head. "This is beyond calm."

They finished their meal, paid the stone faced restaurant owner and walked out on to the empty sidewalk.

"You notice something about the food in there?" Wayne asked as they stood glancing around the oddly quiet town.

"You mean that it was dreadfully bad?" Wyatt asked.

"It wasn't so much bad as utterly tasteless." Wayne said.

"Well, honestly, in a small city like this, I wasn't expecting much anyway." Wyatt said.

"Right, it's almost like it wasn't just bad cooking. It was more like the owner didn't even care what the food tasted like." Wayne said.

"The other patrons didn't seem to mind it." Wyatt said as they walked down the street.

"Yeah. Like they were just going through the motions of eating. Weird." Wayne said.

They stepped down from the sidewalk as they passed an alley between buildings.

"You the government guys?" A voice spoke from the shadows of the alley.

Both Wayne and Wyatt turned towards the voice. Instinctively Wyatt reached inside his jacket and rested his hand on his .45.

"And you would be?" Wayne asked.

The man stepped forward and the light from the street illuminated him.

"Major McMaster." The man was tall, black haired and well built.

Wyatt pulled his hand back out of his jacket.

"Where have you been, Major McMaster? Officials in Washington are concerned." Wayne said.

"I was just doing some investigating. Routine stuff. But everything's fine here." McMaster said flatly.

"Really? Something seems a little odd here." Wyatt commented

McMaster gave a slow shake of his head. "No. You're mistaken. Everything here is fine. You should go back to Washington and let them know I have everything under control here."

"What exactly does that mean?" Wayne asked.

McMaster gave a short shrug. "Everything is fine here. You should go."

Wayne glanced at Wyatt and then back towards McMaster. "I think we need to..."

McMaster slid backwards into the shadows of the alley.

Again Wayne and Wyatt looked at each other. Wayne stepped forward as he lost sight of McMaster. He caught a glimpse of McMaster ducking down the alley and then around a corner.

"What the hell?" Wayne said and moved down the alley. Wyatt was close behind.

They reached the corner where McMaster had disappeared. They scanned the dark area back behind the buildings, but saw no sign of McMaster.

"What the hell was that about?" Wyatt asked.

"Good question." Wayne said. "It seems that whatever has affected these people also has some kind of hold over McMaster."

They walked slowly back to their hotel.

As they crossed the lobby the clerk called out to them in a cheery voice. "Have a nice sleep gentlemen."

Wayne and Wyatt exchanged a mildly confused look, but said nothing. There was an unspoken agreement to not say anything in front of the townspeople. They ascended the stairs and went into their room.

The room was drab and plain with two twin beds, a night stand and a small dresser with a wash basin on it. They sat down on the beds.

"So." Wyatt said. It came out as both a statement and a question.

"Yeah." Wayne answered. "Something strange is going on here, but I'll be damned if I can see it."

"Everything is just fine." Wyatt said, clearly sarcastic. "Just too damn fine."

"Right. Like there's an obsessive need to convince us that everything is just peachy keen." Wayne said.

Wyatt sighed. "I don't know. Maybe things will seem less fine tomorrow and we can get to the bottom of this."

"Maybe." Wayne said. He turned, raised his feet on to the bed and slid up along the bed so his back was against the headboard. Wyatt did the same. This was standard practice when out in the field in a potentially hostile environment.

Wayne slid his .45 out, checked it and laid it on the bed next to him. Wyatt had already done the same. Wayne reached out and turned off the light.

"Why the cheery greeting?" Wyatt asked.

"Huh?" Wayne asked.

"The hotel clerk." Wyatt answered.

"Yeah." Wayne said nodding in the semi-darkness of the room. "That may have been the creepiest thing of the day."

The lights of the street in front of the hotel shone through the sheer curtains of the room. Some of the lights were neon signs and their flickering on and off altered the color of their room moment to moment. Time passed. Wyatt dozed a little. Wayne was lost in thought.

A thump in the room next door brought both of them fully awake. Wyatt had picked up his gun. Wayne sat motionless listening.

Wyatt leaned forward slightly so the street lights lit up his face and turned to look at Wayne. A moment later Wayne's face moved forward into the light. This allowed them to exchange expressions. In this way they could wordlessly communicate to some degree.

There was a muffled sound like footsteps moving away, down the hall. Wayne and Wyatt traded looks of uncertainty. Was that something to be concerned about or nothing at all? Minutes passed. Finally Wayne gestured for Wyatt to check the door to the hallway.

While Wyatt moved to that door Wayne crept over to the door between their room and the next one. Wyatt eased the door to the hall open and peeked out. He turned back and waited for Wayne to look at him. Wyatt shook his head. Wayne nodded.

Slowly Wayne turned the knob of the door between the rooms. This door was typically locked and Wayne was mildly surprised to find it unlocked. When he had turned the knob sufficiently he eased the door slowly open.

The adjoining room was dark—-darker than their room and it was impossible to see much of anything. Wayne turned towards Wyatt and made a hand gesture that Wyatt recognized. Quietly Wyatt retrieved a flashlight from one of their bags moved up next to Wayne.

A cautious sweep around the room with the flashlight didn't reveal anything. Nothing moving. Nothing but a couple more beds. The two of them eased into the room. They walked carefully over to the middle of the room. Still nothing.

There was an odd sound from the floor between the beds. It was hard to define. Like a squishy oozing sound. Wyatt moved the beam of the flashlight to the floor between the beds. They froze. Neither of them moved.

"What the hell?" Wyatt whispered.

"What is it?" Wayne asked.

"I have no idea." Wyatt answered.

"You're the zoologist." Wayne commented.

"Hey, there isn't anything in the animal kingdom that looks like that. Besides, it looks more plantlike than animal." Wyatt said.

They stared at the oblong thing. In the light of the flashlight they could see it was wet or slimy. What ever it was, it was apparently alive. It pulsated as if it were breathing. In the beam of the flashlight it was hard to determine the color of the thing, but it was clearly at least 4 foot long.

There was another squishy sound from the other side of the farthest bed. Wyatt slid to his left and shone the flashlight over there.

"Another one?" Wayne asked.

"Yeah." Was Wyatt curt answer.

"Check around." Wayne suggested.

Wyatt scanned the rest of the room. There weren't any more of them. He moved closer to the thing between the beds.

"Careful." Wayne said.

Wyatt nodded, though it was likely that Wayne couldn't see the nod. As Wyatt held the flashlight out closer to the thing on the floor the light dimly penetrated the exterior of the thing. Inside the thing they could just barely make out a shape.

"If...I didn't know better I'd say that looks like a head..." Wyatt said slowly.

Wayne leaned a little closer. "You know, you're right."

The thing quivered and both Wayne and Wyatt quickly slid backward.

"Let's get out of here." Wayne said.

Wyatt hesitated and then decided that they really didn't know what this thing was or if it was dangerous in some infectious kind of way. They retreated back to their room, closing and locking the door. They stood quietly in the middle of their room for a moment.

"What do you think?" Wayne asked.

"Whatever that thing is it's growing. That much was obvious. In the couple of minutes we watched it I am sure it was slowly expanding." Wyatt said.

"Growing? Into what?" Wayne asked.

Wyatt shook his head. "Don't know. But it's a living growing thing. That I am sure of that. Just not like anything I have ever seen before."

"Kind of coincidental that there was two of them right next door to us." Wayne said looking over at Wyatt.

"Yeah. Kind of is." Wyatt said nodding. "But I'm not sure how it would be related to us."

Wayne shook his head. "Don't know either, but I will bet it's related to why these people in Santa Mira are all acting strange."

"You think these people had something to do with those things being in there?" Wyatt asked.

"Maybe." Wayne replied.

"Well, it's a sure bet that those things didn't check into that room on their own." Wyatt commented.

"I don't think it's safe to stay here." Wayne said.

Wyatt glanced over at the door between the rooms. He was trying to imagine what those things would look like when they were finished growing. "Yeah. Let's not wait around for those things to mature."

They took several minutes to pocket the extra ammunition they had stowed in their luggage and then eased out the door and into the hall. Wayne waved them towards a small side hall. He had noticed it earlier and it led towards the back of the building. The hall ended at a window that overlooked a back alley. Outside the window was a fire escape.

It took a few minutes to quietly force the old window open. When they reached the bottom of the fire escape a rusty ladder waited for them to release it so it would drop to the street below. Wayne glanced at Wyatt and shook his head. Wyatt knew what Wayne was thinking.

If they dropped the ladder, assuming the rust would allow it, the ladder would slide down with what was likely to be a screeching clang.

Wayne hung down from the bottom of the unreleased ladder and dropped remaining eight feet to the pavement below. Wyatt followed. Once down they walked along the back alley until they had moved past several buildings. The alley stopped at a tall wooden fence. Their was no obvious way over it. To their right a narrow alley led back out to the main street of Santa Mira. For a lack of options they began heading back out towards the main street.

"Hey." Wyatt said and pointed up at another fire escape. The ladder was partially lowered. "I think we could reach that."

Wayne glanced up at it. "Maybe with something to stand on."

They looked around. Wyatt moved further up the alley and came back with a couple of crates. They stacked them and Wyatt, on top of the crates, was able pull on the ladder. It didn't move. It seemed to be locked in its current state permanently. With a shrug Wyatt pulled himself up and climbed the ladder until he had reached the steps of the fire escape. As he made his way up the steps Wayne climbed the ladder behind him.

The building was three stories high, but the fire escape stopped at a window on the third floor. It was about ten feet from the flat roof of the building. They stood on the fire escape.

"Where to now? In there?" Wyatt asked and waved towards the window of the building.

Wayne sighed. "Probably just more of the lovely citizens of Santa Mira waiting for us in there. If I'm going to hide out for the night somewhere I'd rather do it up there." He pointed towards the roof.

"Yeah, well, looks like the only way we can do that is if we can shimmy up the drain pipe." Wyatt said.

Wayne reached out to the drain pipe that ran from the roof to the street next to the fire escape. He grabbed a hold of it and shook. The pipe didn't move.

"Seems solid enough." Wayne said. He swung a foot out and began climbing the pipe. Wyatt waited until Wayne had reached the roof before he climbed out on to the pipe.

Once up on the roof of the building they cautiously walked out to the front edge of the roof. It overlooked the main street of Santa Mira. They stood quietly watching the activity of the small city.

"Sure looks normal from up here." Wyatt said.

"Yeah. It does." Wayne agreed.

They could hear sirens moving further up the street in their direction. Instinctively they stepped a little back from the front edge of the roof. A car came speeding along the street. It swung into an alley on the other side of the building, opposite from the side they climbed up. They moved to that edge of the roof. Below the car sped towards the back of the building. Wayne and Wyatt followed along the roof to the back. There was a used car lot at the back of the building. As they watched the car turned into the used car lot and parked. A man and a woman climbed out of the car. The man grabbed a For Sale sign from a nearby car and stuck it on to the car they had just gotten out of. The couple ran, hand in hand, back up the alley and into an adjacent building. Police cars, sirens blaring, zoomed past on the main street.

"Hmm, that's interesting." Wayne said. "They sure seemed afraid of something."

"What's even more interesting, to me, is that their behavior strikes me as the most normal we have seen since we've been here." Wyatt said.

"You're right." Wayne said nodding his head.

They sat down and leaned against the small two foot high wall that ran around the edge of the roof. They were quiet for a few minutes.

"Any more thoughts about what we saw in the hotel?" Wayne asked.

"I was just working through that." Wyatt answered. "It looked...like the form of a human being. The thing in the pod."

Wayne nodded. "I would agree with that, but it doesn't make any sense. That thing was like a giant pea pod."

Wyatt spoke slowly. "Does seem strange. A plant producing some kind of animal."

"Not just an animal, but something resembling a human being." Wayne said.

"Right. As if this town didn't have its own share of weird people." Wyatt spoke the words and, after a moment more, it struck him. His eyes slowly met Wayne's gaze.

"Holy shit." Wayne said.

"Yeah. Yeah. The people of this town aren't...they came out of..." Wyatt was trying to work through it.

"But how?" Wayne asked.

Wyatt shook his head. "I don't know. The cell structure alone would be totally wrong."

"No, I mean, how would they just pop out of these pod things and then, what, get up and just start walking and talking and driving cars?" Wayne asked.

"I agree. Doesn't seem possible. Unless...it wasn't just physical appearance that could be duplicated in the...pod processing." Wyatt said, his mind churning.

"What do you mean? Like they read a person's mind too?" Wayne was struggling to believe any of it was possible.

"I don't know. Maybe. Maybe they can map over everything about the person they are duplicating." Wyatt said.

"That's just crazy. I mean, we've seen a lot of wild stuff before, but this...this is...well, crazy. Who could be behind something like this?" Wayne asked the question more to himself than to Wyatt.

"I think this is beyond anything human beings are capable of." Wyatt said.

Wayne looked over at Wyatt. "What are you saying? This another issue with radiation exposure?"

Wyatt shook his head. "I don't think so. Its not just a mutation of an existing life form. This is some kind of completely new form of life."

"Like the Gill man?" Wayne asked.

Wyatt shook his head. "No. The Gill man was determined to be a variation of the evolutionary process. This doesn't seem like anything in any evolutionary line."

"So, what, maybe Martians?" Wayne clearly didn't believe that.

"I don't know, but there is clearly an organization to these...things. They work together and have some kind of plan." Wyatt said.

Wayne sighed. "Yeah. Does seem like it."

They were quiet for a few minutes.

"So, if they can grow a new person and duplicate a real person, what do they do with the real people? Where are they?" Wayne pondered.

Wyatt nodded. "Good question. Maybe locked up somewhere?"

Wayne nodded also. "Maybe. And if that's true then maybe we should focus on finding the real people."

"I agree." Wyatt said. "We should free them from wherever they are kept and hopefully they can tell us more about what these things are."

"Alright. Well, its a plan. Let's try to get some sleep and maybe at first light we can start looking for the real people of Santa Mira." Wayne said.

4

"Damn. It gets chilly here at night." Wyatt said.

"Its mostly desert here." Wayne replied.

"Guess so. Anyway, its getting light out." Wyatt glanced towards the gray sky to the east.

"I was thinking." Wayne said.

"Is that wise?" Wyatt asked, a smile creeping across his face.

Wayne ignored him. "Everyone hasn't been affected by whatever these pod things are. Those two people we saw last night at the used car lot were clearly not...pod people."

Wyatt nodded. "Yeah. They actually seemed to possess emotions."

"Fear."

"Yeah." Wyatt agreed. "So what are you thinking?"

"Maybe only the people in important positions have been...taken over. Maybe there are more people—-normal people further out from the center of town." Wayne said.

"You think we could recruit some help?" Wyatt asked.

"Yeah." Wayne answered.

"OK. So we head out to the edge of town and see if we can round up a posse." Wyatt said.

"Something like that." Wayne replied.

"And on the way out we need to keep an eye out for some sign of where the actual people of Santa Mira are at." Wyatt said.

Wayne nodded. "Well, I guess we might as well get started."

They got up and, as quietly as possible, climbed back down to the side street below. For the next couple of hours they worked their way through alleys and side streets moving from one bit of cover to the next. Whenever they could not avoid encountering someone they walked stiffly with expressionless faces keeping their words to a minimum and their voices at a monotone. Fortunately they only had to put on that charade twice and, as best they could determine, they got away with it. They stopped behind a shed located at the back of an old hardware store.

"These buildings out this way look more like warehouses." Wyatt observed.

"Yeah." Wayne said. "I think we need to get clear of this area. Probably need to be in a more residential area where the houses are more spread out. I think that's where our best chance to find some non-pod people."

They slid out from behind the shed moved past an old wooden structure, then another building with numerous broken windows that was predominantly empty. They began skirting around a third building that was clearly in better shape than the last two. Wyatt stopped. Wayne turned to look back at Wyatt.

"What?" Wayne asked quietly. He was quickly glancing about under the assumption that Wyatt saw or heard someone.

"Do you smell that?" Wyatt asked.

"Smell?" Wayne looked a little confused.

"Smell." Wyatt said.

Wayne sniffed the air. "Oh. That smells like..."

"Yeah." Wyatt said. "Something rotting."

"There's a door up here." Wayne waved ahead of them. "I'm not sure I want to, but let's have a look."

They crept up to the door and listened for a moment. They didn't hear anything. Wayne tried the door. It was locked. Wayne reached inside his jacket and slid out a small leather case. He unzipped the case and there were several small tools inside. He glanced at the lock and chose a couple. Wayne knelt down and in less than thirty seconds He pulled the door open a little. He listened again, but still heard nothing. He made a face at the smell that wafted out of the door.

With a nod towards Wyatt, Wayne slid inside the building. Wyatt followed. The building was a warehouse. There were large crates and boxes stacked high in front of them. They could only see a short distance ahead because of the crates. To their right, higher up, were some offices. the building was about three stories high and somewhere there must be a set of stairs that took one up to the offices above.

To the left was a narrow passage through the crates. Wayne waved in that direction and Wyatt nodded. They pulled out their .45s and moved cautiously between the crates. They had to zigzag a couple of times as they navigated through the various storage containers before they rounded a corner and stood staring at a relatively clear area that took up about half the space of the warehouse, piled with dead bodies.

Wayne and Wyatt exchanged cold hard looks.

"I guess these were the good people of Santa Mira." Wyatt said quietly.

"Yeah." Wayne's voice was as hard as steel.

"This...isn't some kind of plague or Communist conspiracy." Wyatt said quietly as if a loud voice would somehow disturb the dead lying before them.

Wayne shook his head slowly. "No. Its not. This is organized and deliberate and..."

"Inhuman." Wyatt said.

"Yeah. Inhuman."

Wayne and Wyatt stood staring at the bodies for a long minute. Finally Wayne turned to look at Wyatt.

"Maybe I am optimistic about humanity, but, I think, whatever is behind this...is literally not human in origin." Wayne said.

Wyatt nodded, still staring at the bodies. "I agree. But I'm not sure what that means."

"Have you read the reports we've been getting on the possibility of beings from outer space?" Wayne asked.

Wyatt nodded again. "I have. Not sure what to make of them. They have been largely inconclusive."

Wyatt turned to look at Wayne. "You think that's what's behind this? Some kind of space alien invasion?"

Wayne shrugged. "Don't know. But whoever is behind this doesn't have any humanity in them."

"So...the people of Santa Mira...are not humans—-at least that's our working theory at the moment." Wyatt said.

Wayne nodded. "Yeah. That's what I am thinking."

In the distance a loud siren started wailing with an odd honking sound to it. There seemed to be some kind of commotion going on from somewhere in the nearby streets of Santa Mira. In wordless agreement Wayne and Wyatt eased around the pile of bodies to the far side of the warehouse. They moved to a door and slipped out of it. To their right they heard the sound of scuffling feet. The further up the street they glimpsed a couple running. It looked to them to be the same couple they had seen the night before in the used car lot.

Rounding a bend in the street Wayne and Wyatt lost sight of the couple. Moments later they briefly spotted them again climbing a set of steps leading up a hillside at the edge of town. A police siren could be heard now approaching from their left, the direction of the main street of Santa Mira. In addition, there was the sound of running feet—-lots of running feet.

With a quick glance at each other Wayne and Wyatt ducked back into the warehouse. Less than a minute later a police car and then a large group of people came rushing past the warehouse. Wayne and Wyatt watched them through a dirty window next to the door.

"That couple." Wyatt said.

"I know. They must still be human." Wayne answered.

"We need to help them." Wyatt reached for the door, but Wayne stopped him.

"There's no way we are going to catch up with them now. Not before that mob gets to them. Even if we did, I don't think we have enough firepower to stop that many pod people." Wayne explained.

"We need to stop this." Wyatt said.

"I agree, but we're going to need a lot more help." Wayne said. "We need to get word out to the military."

"There may be more people here in Santa Mira that are still human." Wyatt said.

"Maybe so, but someone has to get out of here and warn the outside world about what's happening here. If none of us get out then this will just spread." Wayne said. "We are probably the best equipped individuals left to make it out of here."

Wyatt stood quietly for a moment. He was clearly working through the logic of their situation.

"OK. Let's go. The sooner we get help in here the more lives we can save." Wyatt said with a sigh.

"Agreed." Wayne said. He eased the door open slowly and peeked out into the street beyond. With a nod to Wyatt, the two of them slid out, guns still in hand, and moved quietly and carefully down the street.

5

Wyatt reached out and put a hand on Wayne's arm. "There." He whispered and pointed down along the street. They remained crouched behind some trash bins on a side street.

Wayne saw the man. He was standing next to a dumpster. There was smoke slowly lifting out of the dumpster.

"What do you think?' Wyatt asked softly.

Wayne shrugged. "Not sure, but we need to get past him to get down that other side street."

"Well, maybe if we just look like we're busy doing something we can slip past him." Wyatt suggested.

"Worth a try, I guess." Wayne said slowly standing up and walking nonchalantly down the street towards the man at the dumpster. Wyatt followed along.

As they drew near to the man he looked up and spotted them. He stared at them for a moment.

"Were you sent to help me with this?" The man gestured towards the dumpster.

"Uh, no. We have something else we have to get done." Wayne said as he and Wyatt kept walking until they were close to the dumpster and the man.

"Someone was supposed to help me with this." The man stated flatly.

"Not us. Ugh!" Wyatt reached up and covered his nose. Wayne was turning his head away from the smell of whatever was burning in the dumpster. The smell was making both of them struggle not to vomit.

The man stared at them quizzically. Slowly his expression changed to a scowl.

"Hey." The man said as Wayne and Wyatt picked up their pace and quickly moved past the man.

"Hey!" The man said again. "Stop! You two stop!"

Wayne stopped and turned to look at the man. "There's no problem here." He tried to keep his voice as toneless as possible.

The man looked at them suspiciously and then turned towards the end of the street they had just come from.

"Hey!" The man yelled. "There's two down here!"

Wayne pulled his gun out and pointed it at the man. "Quiet. I don't want to have to use this, but I will if you force me to."

"Down here!" The man yelled again. He didn't seem the slightest bit intimidated by the gun.

"I said shut up!" Wayne rasped sharply at the man. Two people, a man and a woman, rounded the far corner of the street. They watched for a moment and then, as the man at the dumpster waved for them to come, they started hustling down the street.

"Dammit!" Wayne shot the man.

The man stumbled backwards. Despite a bullet straight into the chest the man did not cry out and even started getting back up off the ground.

"What the hell?" Wyatt asked watching the man.

Wayne fired another shot that took off part of the back of the man's head, but still the man seemed to be intent on standing up.

The two people coming up the street started calling out and a third and then a fourth person came around the corner into the street they were in.

"We need to go." Wayne said.

"Yeah." Wyatt said joining Wayne in a sprint away from the man and the dumpster fire.

They reached the side street they were trying to get to and ducked into it. They could hear the shouts of what sounded like quite a crowd now behind them somewhere in pursuit. As they reached a cross street they heard the mob pursuing them rushing down the street they were on.

"This way." Wayne said turning left into another street.

"Maybe we could dissuade them from following us with a few shots." Wyatt suggested.

"Somehow I doubt it. They don't seem to worried about being shot or killed—-if that's even possible." Wayne replied.

"Yeah, well, after that warehouse, it wouldn't break my heart to try." Wyatt said.

"I agree, but the truth is we don't have enough bullets to shoot everyone in this town." Wayne pointed out.

"Especially if they don't seem to want to die very easily like our dumpster friend." Wyatt said.

"Yeah. Wait. Over there." Wayne pointed at a gas station. "I have an idea."

They angled across the street towards the gas station as the crowd behind them rounded the corner and were now within sight of them.

Wayne ran up to a gas pump. "Go find some matches or a lighter." He waved towards the gas station.

Wyatt ran into the gas station office and started scrounging around. In the meantime, Wayne was busy pumping gas out on to the pavement. The stream of gas was running out into the street. By the time Wyatt returned a large quantity of gas had spread out across the gas station pavement and in the street—-conveniently flowing in the general direction of the approaching mob. They didn't seem to grasp the developing situation or they just didn't care. They continued on in a mad rush towards Wayne and Wyatt.

Wayne looked at Wyatt questioningly.

Wyatt held up a wrench.

"That's not a match or a lighter." Wayne said, a hint of concern in his voice as the crowd drew nearer.

"Actually, its kind of a lighter." Wyatt walked out to the edge of the gas flow. He bent down and banged the wrench on the cement. Nothing happened. He banged it down twice more and still nothing.

"As I said, not a..." Wayne started.

With another clang on to the cement a spark shot out and ignited the gas. A moment later there was a wall of flame shooting across the gas station and down the street. Wyatt threw the wrench towards the approaching people and actually struck one of them in the chest. The impact seemed to have little impact, but the leading edge of the crowd was suddenly engulfed in flame and the others behind them staggered back.

"Let's go." Wayne said and the both of them turned and sped down another side street. After a couple more turns they stopped and listened. They could hear shouts in the distance, but no sounds of pursuers.

They moved carefully through several more streets in the general direction of where they knew the interstate was, somewhere in the distance. Time passed and they said very little other than to comment on the best route to follow. A couple of times they were almost spotted by what passed in Santa Mira as people shuffling along the streets.

Wayne stopped. Wyatt stopped as well and looked over at Wayne.

Wayne sighed. "The interstate is still quite a distance out that way." He pointed.

Wyatt nodded slightly. "Yeah."

"At this rate..." Wayne trailed off.

"I know. I was thinking the same thing. By the time we make it out of here on foot these...people...things could have spread all over the place." Wyatt said.

"We need to get us some transportation." Wayne said.

"Agreed." Wyatt said.

Wayne waved back slightly behind them. "There were more houses back over there. We might be able to find an abandoned car somewhere there."

Wyatt nodded and the two of them turned back and made their way through some quieter streets. The houses further back away from the main street through Santa Mira were nearly all dark. There seemed to be little or no activity going on back here.

"There." Wayne said quietly and pointed at a dark house with a short driveway in front of it. There was a car parked in the drive. The two of them crossed the street at a place where the aging streetlight only dimly lit the black pavement.

Wayne checked the driver's side door. It was unlocked. He opened the door and got down on his knees. Wayne felt around under the steering column.

"This would be a lot easier with a little light." Wayne said still fumbling around trying to feel the wires under the dash board.

"Yeah or maybe just a...wait." Wyatt said turning his head and listening.

Wayne pulled his head back out of the car. He looked up at Wyatt.

"What is it?" Wayne whispered.

Wyatt held up a hand for a moment. He tilted his head a little and then gestured towards a neighboring house.

"I think I hear someone. Not sure." Wyatt said in a hushed voice.

Wayne sat quietly for a minute, but then shook his head. "Don't hear anything."

Wyatt tapped Wayne on the shoulder. "Keep working on the car. I'm going to check it out."

"Careful." Wayne said.

"Right." Wyatt said and eased around the car.

There was a wooden solid fence separating the house where the car was and the next one. Wyatt walked to the fence and listened. He could still faintly hear the sound, but still couldn't identify it. Moving in the general direction of where he thought it was coming from he crept along the fence towards the back of the house.

When Wyatt reached the backyard of the house he could now distinctly hear the muffled sounds of a person. He still couldn't tell what they were saying—-if what he was hearing were words at all. He hesitated for a moment, but the sound had an emotional quality to it and, from what he had experienced in Santa Mira, the "things" here seemed to be lacking any real emotion. Trusting his instinct Wyatt reached up to the top of the fence and pulled himself over it.

There was a frightened gasp as Wyatt landed on the other side. A woman was kneeling on the ground in the middle of her backyard. She had scrambled sideways slightly as Wyatt suddenly appeared only a few feet away.

The woman awkwardly grabbed a baseball bat near her and weakly swung it in Wyatt's direction.

Wyatt froze and then slowly eased down to one knee. He realized the woman had been kneeling here and crying. "It's OK. I'm not going to hurt you."

The woman just stared at him still holding the bat between them.

Wyatt thought for a moment. "I'm not one of them."

The woman stared at Wyatt for a long minute.

"You...don't act like one of them." The woman said.

"Do you know what they are? How they got here?" Wyatt asked.

The woman shook her head. "No. We didn't know they were even here. People just started changing. And...and..." The woman stared down at the ground next to her.

Wyatt studied the ground in front of the woman. There was some churned up dirt. Like someone had been digging something up. Wyatt shifted slightly to allow the weak light from the street to drape across the ground. It was more than just loose dirt. There was a shoe half buried in the pile.

It took Wyatt a moment more to realize that there was a foot inside the shoe. He glanced over at the woman. He could see her face better and recognized that she was in her late teens or early twenties. She was still watching him.

Wyatt looked down at the foot sticking out of the dirt and then back to the girl.

The girl hesitated and then seemed to decide something. "My brother."

"They killed him?" Wyatt asked.

The girl shook her head. Her voice was distant. "I killed him."

"OK..." Wyatt said. He was sure this girl wasn't one of the pod people things because of how she acted, but he wasn't sure she was still sane—-also because of how she acted.

"He was my brother, but not my brother." The girl said.

"Ah, yeah. I understand." Wyatt said, feeling a little more at ease. "Listen, I am an OSO agent and—-"

"A what?" The girl asked.

"Uh, I'm a government agent. My partner and I are here to...well, sort this whole mess out." Wyatt said. He wasn't sure what to tell the girl. It wasn't like he and Wayne were on the verge of saving the town of Santa Mira.

"Oh." The girl didn't seem that interested.

Wyatt understood. Whatever "sorting out" he and Wayne did wasn't going to bring this girl's brother back or erase the memory this girl had of killing something that looked exactly like her brother.

"You should come with us. We will get you out of here." Wyatt stood up and held out his hand.

The girl stared at him for a full minute. Finally, she stood up, still holding her bat. She didn't take Wyatt's hand, but slowly followed him as they walked back towards the street. Wyatt had decided he wasn't going to ask the girl to climb over the fence.

6

Wayne was pretty sure this time he had the correct wires. He twisted slightly trying to get a little light to shine into the car, but it was to no avail. He had finished stripping the ends of the wires and was about to see if they would spark when he heard a sound moving up along side the car.

"Did you find out what the sound was?" Wayne asked without looking up.

"You should stand up." The voice was not Wyatt's. It was much older and gravelly sounding.

Wayne looked up to see an old man standing a short distance away—-pointing a shotgun at him.

"You should stand up." The old man said. There was no emotion or inflection in his voice at all.

Wayne stood up slowly. He put his hands up.

The man leaned forward slightly staring at Wayne. "You have a gun. You put that down on the ground."

Wayne wondered how fast he could turn the gun towards the man and get off a shot. Fast enough to avoid having a hole blown into him by the shotgun? He didn't think so. He slid the gun out and dropped it.

The old man waved the gun. "In the house."

They walked up the front steps and through the screen door. The man directed Wayne down a short hallway. They stopped half way down the hall, next to a door. At the man's direction Wayne opened the door and flipped a switch on the wall. There were wooden steps leading down into a basement.

"Go on." The man said.

Wayne walked down the steps. He had to duck his head at the bottom of the steps because of the low ceiling of the basement.

The basement door slammed shut and Wayne could here a lock being turned.

"There's something down there for you." The man said through the door.

Wayne glanced around. About 7 feet to his left was a pod. He stared at it. Even from this distance he could see the slight rippling of the sides of the pod. It was as if the thing was breathing. He glanced around for something he could use to destroy, but the basement was devoid anything except dust and cob webs.

Wayne backed up a few feet. He wasn't sure how this process worked, but he thought keeping some distance between himself and the pod wouldn't hurt. Suddenly the light went out.

"That's not good." Wayne said quietly to himself.

The girl, Emily, followed behind Wyatt as he walked back up the drive towards the car Wayne was trying to get started. She had long brown hair and wasn't very tall. Other than giving Wyatt her name she didn't say much.

Wyatt stopped a few feet away from the open driver's side door of the car. He just stared at the scene. Wayne was nowhere to be seen. More importantly, his gun lay on the ground next to the car. No OSO agent was ever voluntarily separated from his gun.

Wyatt glanced around. Everything seemed still and quiet. He reached down and picked up Wayne's gun and tucked it into the waistband of his pants. He drew his own gun out. Wyatt scanned the house. There was a dim light coming from somewhere further in the house. The house had been completely dark when they had first arrived.

"What's wrong?" Emily asked.

"My partner. He's missing." Wyatt said. "Wait here."

Emily did not respond. Wyatt was about to turn around and make sure Emily heard him when he noticed that someone had come out of the house. Wyatt could not see the figure very well, but he felt certain it was a man. Wyatt stepped around the door of the car and a step closer to the house. He stopped when he noticed the shotgun in the man's hands.

The two of them stood for a moment in silence. Their respective guns pointed at each other.

"Where is my partner?" Wyatt asked the man.

"Your friend is gone." The man answered.

"I don't think so. He wouldn't leave without me." Wyatt replied.

"Maybe he didn't leave the way you think." The man said.

Wyatt thought about that. It occurred to him what the man was saying. Angered stirred in Wyatt at the thought that Wayne could have been turned into one of those pod people. If that were true Wyatt decided he would kill this man-pod thing in front of him—-shotgun be damned.

Wyatt took a step forward towards the man intent on putting a bullet through his skull. There was a solid thump and Wyatt watched the man dropped the shotgun and fall face first down the front steps. Standing behind the man was Emily still firmly gripping her baseball bat.

Wyatt stared at her.

Emily looked back. "I never liked Old Man Grissom even before he changed into one of those things."

"Uh, right." Wyatt said and joined Emily on the front porch. He eased past Emily and through the front door. He held his .45 in front of him in case there were other pod-people somewhere inside skulking about. Wyatt wasn't sure pod-people skulked much, but he was going to be ready nonetheless.

Wyatt walked into a small musty-smelling living room and stood listening. He didn't hear anything.

"Thomas?" No answer.

"Who is Thomas?" Emily's voice came from behind Wyatt.

"My partner." Wyatt answered.

"Hey, anyone here?" Emily yelled.

Wyatt turned around and looked at Emily. "I was trying not to attract attention."

Emily shrugged. "Can't stay here all night."

There was a muffled voice coming from somewhere. Wyatt and Emily both heard the voice and exchanged looks. It was obvious that neither one could tell where the sound came from.

"Thomas!" Wyatt shouted out.

This time the voice was a little more distinct. It was clearly a voice calling back the word: "Here."

Emily waved Wyatt towards the hallway running through the middle of the house. They moved into the hall. Wyatt glanced at a door part way down the hall. He went over to it and banged once on it.

"Down here." Came Wayne's distant voice.

Wyatt tried the door. It was locked, but he could tell the door was, like everything else in the house, showing its age. He waved for Emily to step back and then gave the door a kick. The door remained intact, but it was apparent even after one kick that the door was not going to hold back Wyatt's foot indefinitely.

Three more solid kicks and enough of the door had given way to allow Wyatt to wedge his way through.

"Wait here." Wyatt said. He took a step and then pulled Wayne's gun out. He set it down on a small table near the door of the basement. He looked at Emily.

"Just in case there's any trouble up here." Wyatt said indicating the gun.

Emily nodded.

"You know how to use one of them?" Wyatt asked.

Emily nodded again. "I shot a few rattlesnakes before."

"Keep an eye out." Wyatt said to Emily over his shoulder as he slid through the broken door. Carefully Wyatt made his way down the creaking basement steps.

"Careful." Came Wayne's voice. "There's one of those pod things down here."

"OK. Not really enough light coming through the door to see much." Wyatt said.

"Somewhere up there must be a light switch." Wayne said.

Wyatt turned slightly, still on the steps. "Emily, see if you can find a light switch up there."

"OK." Came a voice.

"Who's Emily?" Wayne asked.

"A neighbor." Wyatt replied.

"The someone you thought you heard?" Wayne asked.

"The same." Wyatt answered.

"A non-pod person I assume." Wayne said.

The basement lights came on.

"Uh, yeah, a...non-pod." Wyatt said continuing on down the stairs.

Wayne gestured towards the pod. It was about the same size as a person.

Wyatt stared at it for a moment. "Creepy. Seems like we ought to do something about it before we leave here."

Wayne nodded slightly. "I was thinking the same thing. Couldn't find anything down here to do the job and I wasn't sure getting near it was wise."

"Probably a good idea not to get too close." Wyatt held up his gun. "What do think? Might draw attention if anyone hears it."

Wayne shrugged. "It might, but it might be useful to know if it could be killed."

Wyatt nodded. And after that warehouse I kind of feel like doing it out of..." His voiced trailed of a little.

Wayne nodded. "I agree. Fire away."

Wyatt fired three shots into the pod. Fluid oozed out of the holes. There were several significant convulsions from the pod and then the movement that seemed like breathing stopped.

"Go to know." Wayne said. They both turned around at the sound of scrambling on the stairs. It was Emily. She stood on the stairs holding the .45.

Wayne and Wyatt stared at Emily.

"Uh...no rattlesnakes down here." Wyatt started.

"I heard shots." Emily said.

"My gun." Wayne said.

"I thought something was happenging." Emily explained.

"We should go." Wayne suggested. He walked to the steps and held out his hand.

Emily handed the gun to Wayne.

"Thomas Wayne. Nice to meet you." Wayne said holstering his gun.

"Likewise." Emily said.

They went back out to the car and Wayne got it started. Slowly Wayne backed the car out on to the street. He hesitated.

"We need to find a way to communicate with the outside world." Wayne said.

"That means getting far enough away to be out of the area controlled by these pod things." Wyatt said.

"Well, you can't go west. There's no road going over the mountains that way." Emily said. "And north there's nothing but desert for a hundred miles. The interstate is south. That goes to Los Angeles."

"They'll probably be watching that." Wyatt said.

"Agreed." Wayne said.

"You could take the county road east. It winds through the hills, but comes out at Salt Springs. Maybe 20 miles." Emily volunteered.

"Sounds like the best option." Wyatt said.

"That means cutting back through the city, though." Wayne pointed out. He turned to look at Emily in the back seat. "Can you get us through the city on back streets?"

Emily nodded. "Sure. Take a right at the stop sign up there." She waved up the street.

7

"I thought you said there wasn't anything out here until Salt Springs." Wayne said staring at the road ahead.

Emily, who had been dozing slightly in the passenger seat, perked up a little. "There isn't." She said almost mumbling.

"Then what's all the lights over there from?" Wayne pointed to a ridge ahead of them and a little off to the left.

Emily shook herself and rubbed her face. She stared at the sky above the ridge. There was a glow coming from the other side of it. She focused and stared at it. She shook her head.

"I don't know." She hesitated. "Wait, I think there used to be an old agricultural station out here, but it hasn't been used in years."

"Yeah, well it looks like the road goes right—-whoa." Wayne said. He braked the car to a stop and turned the lights off.

"What?" Wyatt said. He had been asleep in the backseat and now leaned forward.

"Looks like a road block." Wayne said.

"Did they see us?" Wyatt asked.

"I don't think so." Wayne replied.

"Kind of makes you think there's something going on out here." Wyatt said.

"It does." Wayne said. He turned the car off. "Might be worth taking a look."

"What? Why? I thought we were just trying to get out of here." Emily said irritably.

"We are, but any information we can pass on to the police or military about what's going on here would be useful." Wayne explained.

Wayne and Wyatt climbed out of the car. Emily followed slowly.

"Up there." Wayne waved towards the top of the ridge across the road from them.

"Agreed." Wyatt said. He turned to Emily. "You can wait here if you want."

Emily just shrugged.

Wayne and Wyatt picked their way in the dim light up to the top of the ridge. They crawled the last few feet to the edge and peered over. Below there was a group of buildings surrounded by fence that was clearly in need of repair. The buildings too were showing the desert elements had spent some years wearing them into a shabby state. Despite the condition of the facility there was a buzz of activity going on all around the place.

In the two largest buildings there were bright lights pushing out a streaming glow from every crack in the corrugated steel sides of each building. They seemed to be the center of focus of the people bustling about. At the far end of the buildings there were trucks backed up to what was presumably loading docks. That side of the buildings was out of sight from the ridge top.

"What do you think?" Wayne asked.

Wyatt stared for another moment before answering. "I would guess some kind of processing plant. Like the warehouse in town."

"But bigger." Wayne said.

"A lot bigger." Wyatt said.

"Bigger than what?"

Both Wayne and Wyatt spun around startled.

Emily looked at them. She waved towards the facility below. "That's bigger than what?"

"Bigger than a place back in Santa Mira." Wyatt said.

"You think they're making more pod people in there?" Emily asked.

Wyatt shook his head. "Seems like they need an existing human to create a pod person. Where would they get the people for that out here?"

"Good question." Wayne said still watching the facility.

Wayne and Wyatt exchanged a look.

"Right. We're going to need to take a look." Wyatt said.

"Yeah." Wayne said.

"Look at what?" Emily asked.

"Stay here." Wyatt said.

Wayne and Wyatt made their way along ridge a short ways until they found a slight bend in the ridge that would hide their descent down towards the facility below. They moved slowly and steadily in order to not cause much, if any, rocks rolling down the slope and alerting any of what they assumed were all pod people.

They squatted outside the fence next to a spot where a section of fence hung loosely from the eight poles it was attached to. There were many gaps in the fence like the one they were next to that would easily accommodate a person. They glanced around the area, but saw no one near them. Everyone seemed to be concentrated on the far side of the buildings where the trucks were.

"Not much for security are they?" Wyatt observed.

"With the road block up there they probably don't believe anyone would be out here." Wayne said.

They drew their guns out and slid inside the fence. They moved up to the back of one of the large buildings.

"Over there." Wayne said quietly and pointed towards an opening about the size of a person's head in the corrugated metal. They moved to their left and Wayne stared through the hole for a full minute. He pulled his head back and let Wyatt get a look inside.

"What do think?" Wayne asked Wyatt when he pulled his head back form the hole in the wall.

"Definitely processing something in there." Wyatt answered.

"A different way to make pod people?" Wayne asked.

Wyatt shook his head. "I don't think so. Those tables..."

"There's lots of them in there." Wayne commented.

"Yeah. They have sides to them. Like they're meant for holding something inside of them." Wyatt said.

"You mean like garden bed?" Wayne asked.

"Not so much a garden bed as a shallow tank. Did you notice that some of them were dripping at the corners?" Wyatt said.

Wayne glanced into the hole again. "Didn't see that before. What do you think it is?" He was counting on Wyatt's background in zoology.

"Hard to say without sampling it. But the smell." Wyatt said.

"Yeah. That reeks. Any ideas?" Wayne asked.

"Sorry, no idea. But its biological in nature. It reminds me of placental fluid." Wyatt said.

"Hey, I can't see."

Wayne and Wyatt spun around, guns ready.

Emily stared at their guns. She pointed past the guns at the hole. "I can't see."

"What the hell?" Wayne stared at Emily. He was slower than Wyatt to lower his gun. As if he was having a passing thought.

Emily pushed past the two of them and stuck her head in front of the hole.

Wayne sighed. He looked at Wyatt. "Placental fluid?"

Wyatt thought for a moment. "Right...maybe not growing pod people, but the pod itself. Before it reaches the point of growing a new person it must start out as something smaller. Some kind of proto-pod."

Emily sat back and stared at the hole in the wall.

"Yeah. That makes sense." Wayne said.

"Kill them." Emily said. Her voice was distant.

"What?" Wayne asked.

"We should kill them all." Emily said. "They killed my brother."

"We can't kill them all. There's too many of them." Wayne said.

Wyatt was silent for a moment. "You know, maybe we don't need to kill them all. Just slow them down a bit. I'll be honest with you," Wyatt looked over at Wayne, "I wouldn't mind hurting these bastards a bit myself. They have killed a lot of people."

Wayne thought about it for a minute or two. "Yeah, they kind of pissed me off too."

"Good. Do I get a gun too?" Emily asked.

"Slow down there, Wyatt Earp. First, I don't have a spare gun and second, I don't think shooting a few of them will change much." Wayne turned to Wyatt. "Any ideas?"

Wyatt waved towards the building. "I'm pretty sure I saw a tanker truck parked on the other side."

"To fuel up the trucks." Wayne nodded.

"Presumably." Wyatt agreed.

"But if we wanted to set fire to one of these buildings, how do we get the fuel from the truck to the building?" Wayne asked. He eased to the corner of the building and peered around it. He could see the tanker parked about 100 yards away. There was no cover close to to the tanker and numerous pod-people moving about near it.

Wyatt joined Wayne at the corner of the building. He studied the situation as well. After a couple of minutes Wyatt shook his head.

"I don't see us burning this place down. The buildings are too big and there's too much open space between the tanker truck and the buildings." Wyatt said.

Wayne nodded. "I agree. No way we could transport enough gas from that truck and soak enough parts of those buildings without getting caught."

"I don't think we can..." Wyatt turned to say something to Emily. He just assumed she had followed them over to the corner of the building. She wasn't behind them. Wyatt didn't see her anywhere along the back of the building. "Shit."

Wayne turned around. He glanced around. "The girl."

"Gone." Wyatt said disgustedly. "I will find her." Wyatt started to move back along the building and stopped. He turned back to Wayne.

"We can't really do much here, but we could probably use a distraction. To get her out of here." Wyatt said.

Wayne looked back at Wyatt and then back towards the tanker truck. "Maybe I can arrange something."

Wyatt turned and moved to the far corner of the building. He peered around it. On this side of the building were large piles of what looked like mulch and earth piled up against the fence. backed up to the piles were several pickup trucks. There were a few pod-people working on shoveling the mulch stuff into the back of the trucks. Wyatt didn't see Emily.

A motion of something from between two of the trucks caught Wyatt's eye. It was the end of a shovel raising up and then swinging quickly down again. It happened several times. It was like someone was beating the ground with the shovel. A moment later Wyatt had an ugly idea of what he was seeing. He decided to take a closer look. He scampered, keeping low, towards the pickup trucks making sure the trucks remained between him and the shoveling pod-people.

"Hey! Who are you? What are you doing?"

Wyatt was crouched in front of the truck. He looked around. He couldn't see anyone and was confused at how anyone could see him. He slid up to look over the hood of the truck. He could see through the windshield a pod-person circling around the back of the truck. Wyatt eased to the front passenger side of the truck. He glanced around the corner of the truck.

It was a frightening scene. Emily had just finished pummeling a pod-person into a nasty mess on the ground between a couple of the trucks. She seemed mesmerized by what she had just done and was ignoring the pod-person that was moving towards her. The pod-person raised his shovel up to strike Emily, but she remained oblivious.

Wyatt stood up and stepped around the front of the truck. He swung his .45 out and fired past Emily's head. The bullet ripped through the pod-person's throat. A loud gurgling sound came out of the pod-person. The other two pod-people who were shoveling and had already been watching what was going on started running towards where Emily and Wyatt now stood.

As another pod-person came around the back of a truck and into view Wyatt put a bullet into the creature's head.

"Let's go!" Wyatt yelled to Emily. A heartbeat passed before Emily looked up at Wyatt.

"Come on!" Wyatt called to Emily and held out his hand.

Emily dropped the shovel and ran to Wyatt. The remaining shoveling pod-person appeared at the back of the truck. Wyatt whipped off a shot that hit the pod-person in the leg. The pod-person stumbled and Wyatt and Emily started running back towards the back of the building they had been hiding behind.

They had only covered a few strides when a group of pod-people came running from somewhere in front of the building. They carried a range of different tools and a couple of them had shotguns. Wyatt glanced back at them and didn't like their odds.

From somewhere on the other side of the building Wyatt heard the sound of gun shots. Several shots. He was pretty sure from the sound of the shots they were from a .45. Moments later there was a boom and a sudden whooshing sound. For just an instant there was flicker of orange light. Wyatt knew what that was. Wayne had found a way to blow up the tanker truck.

Wyatt and Emily ducked back around the back corner of the warehouse at about the same time Wayne came sliding in the gravel around the opposite corner.

Wyatt waved back towards the corner of the building they had just come around. "There's pod people coming."

Wayne pointer back behind him. "Here too."

"I think we need to run." Wyatt said.

"Agreed." Wayne answered.

Wyatt grabbed Emily by the forearm and began running towards the fence they had squeezed through earlier. Emily didn't need any encouragement. She was well aware of their situation now. Wayne closely followed them.

They reached the fence at about the time two groups of pod-people appeared from both sides of the warehouse, merged together and continued pursuing them. Emily, Wyatt and Wayne pushed through the gap in the fence and began running as fast as the desert gravel and uneven ground would allow them to.

Wyatt glanced behind them. The pursuing pod-people were still coming, but some of them had turned around and headed back towards the warehouse. He wasn't sure why, but it seemed like less pursuers was better than more.

It took them a little while to scramble back to where they had left their car. Sometime during the race back they had noticed that the pod-people had abandoned the chase. It was a relief, but, as they stood by the car, it turned out to be short-lived.

"Car!" Emily said grabbing Wyatt's arm and pointing in the direction of the gate to the warehouse complex.

"They knew where we were likely heading to." Wyatt said.

"Yeah. Let's get out of here." Wayne said sliding behind the steering wheel.

"There's truck full of them too." Emily said still pointing as Wyatt pushed her into the car.

Wayne got the car turned around as fast as he could and sped back towards Santa Mira.

"This isn't really getting us out of this place." Wyatt commented.

"Yeah." Wayne said. "We're going to have to come up with a plan B."

Wyatt sighed. "I feel like we are already on Plan G."

"Does feel that way." Wayne said.

"I think they're getting closer." Emily said from the back seat as she stared back at the vehicles behind them.

Wayne tried to speed up, but there few warning signs out here about sharp corners and such things and he nearly sent them off the road more than once.

Wayne shook his head a little. "They know the roads out here better than I do."

They were coming back into Santa Mira now and Wayne was forced to slow down some. There were street corners, other cars and, occasionally, people in the roadway. Wayne wasn't opposed to running over pod-people, assuming everyone here was now one of them, but hitting someone would likely send their car crashing into something else. As it turned out running over a pod-person was not the only way to crash the car. In an attempt to take a corner fast, since their pursuers had closed the distance now to them, the tires of the car couldn't grip the road good enough the their car slid sideways into a tree up on the sidewalk.

For a moment time paused as the car stopped dead and the three of them bounced off the interior of the car. Other than being a little stunned they were OK and climbed out of the wrecked car. They were huddled against the side of the car as several vehicles screeched to stop nearby. Pod-people piled out of the other vehicles.

Wayne and Wyatt exchanged a look. They drew out there .45s.

"What's going to happen?" Emily said, fear overwhelming her voice.

Wyatt took a deep breath and let it out slow. "We're going to kill them."

"All of them?" Emily asked.

"As many as we can." Wayne answered her.

"What happens if you can't kill them all?" Emily asked.

Neither Wayne or Wyatt answered.

"I'm not going to become one of them." Emily said with veiled anger in her voice. She grabbed Wyatt's arm. "Promise me you won't let them get me—alive."

Wyatt looked straight at Emily. He could see she was both terrified and determined.

Wyatt nodded slightly. "I won't."

Wayne and Wyatt braced themselves for the coming onslaught and took aim.

8

They had no real cover and hunkered down next to a wrecked car. The crowd formed slightly down and across the street. Wyatt estimated there was between 30 and 40 of them. Too many to get them all with their .45s, but, at this point, there was little left for them to do.

Several of the pod-people wielded guns, pistols, hunting rifles or shotguns. Most carried whatever had been handy at the time they were called to hunt down Wayne, Wyatt and Emily. Usually it was some kind of club—-baseball bats, boards or tools of some kind. Others had various knives like from a butcher shop or ones they found just laying around in a kitchen. One held a sword which, even in this circumstance, seemed odd.

Wayne, Wyatt and Emily waited for the rush. They knew that the crowd would rush them knowing that Wayne and Wyatt would kill some of them before they could reach them, but these creatures didn't seem to value life much. Even their own.

Minutes passed and as the tension grew every second seemed like it would be the one when all hell broke loose. When it appeared the crowd was about to launch their rush something seemed to stir in their ranks. Wayne and Wyatt watched increasingly puzzled about what was holding them back.

The sound of vehicles from somewhere up the street could be heard, but Wayne, Wyatt and Emily could not see who else was coming to join the party because the wrecked car blocked their view in that direction. Tires squealed to a stop and Wyatt shook his head at the thought of how many more of these pod-people they would be facing now.

The crowd across the street were clearly getting agitated and excited. They were looking up the street and they seemed to be changing their formation to face more in that direction.

"What's going on?" Emily asked.

"I don't know, but—-" It was all Wyatt could get out before the gunfire started. A couple of shotguns and a rifle from the crowd fired in the direction of the newly arrived vehicles. What was returned was a fury of gunfire and the pod-people crowd immediately started dropping. They had been bunched together and that meant that few bullets fired into the crowd were missing a target.

Wayne, Wyatt and Emily crouched down as low as they could as the hail of bullets flew past them. They could see the crowd, those not already dead on the ground, were scattering back further into to Santa Mira like rats fleeing to the dark corners of a warehouse.

"Get up! Get Up!" The voice yelled at Wayne, Wyatt and Emily.

They looked up and saw a state trooper standing over them with a pump-action shotgun pointed at them. Wayne and Wyatt set their guns down on the ground and slowly stood up with their hands up.

"Glad you could join us." Wyatt said with a smile.

"Oh thank God!" Emily said, also smiling.

The trooper didn't move. He kept the gun trained on them. A man came up beside the trooper. He was a middle age man in a rumpled suit. He stared at Wyatt and Emily. In particular, at their smiling faces.

"These people are OK." He said. "They aren't part of it."

The trooper nodded, lowered his shotgun and turned moving off further up the street. The man in the rumpled suit studied them for a moment.

"I don't recognize you. Are you from Santa Mira?" The man asked.

Wyatt stepped forward. "I'm Jonathon Wyatt and this is Thomas Wayne. We're from the OSO. The Office of Scientific Operations. We were investigating a missing Air Force Major when we...well, we stumbled into something else."

"OSO...? Office of...?" The man waved his own questions off. "Never mind. I'm Miles Bennell. I'm the—-"

"Doctor Bennell?" Emily asked.

Bennell nodded. "Yeah. Do I know you?"

"My Mother..." Emily hesitated, then went on, "she went to you a couple of times. I'm Emily Hamilton."

Bennell hesitated. "Jennie Hamilton?"

Emily nodded.

"Your her daughter?" Bennell asked.

Emily nodded again.

"Is...she still...?" Bennell faltered.

Emily shook her. She couldn't get the words out. It was obvious that all of this was now catching up to her.

Bennell stepped forward. He put his arm around her. "I'm sorry. I know. I know. We lost a lot of people here."

Bennell started leading Emily away. He looked over at Wayne and Wyatt and nodded a goodbye to them. Emily took a few steps and stopped. She turned back towards Wayne and Wyatt.

"Thank you." She said with tears in her eyes. It was all she could get out.

Wyatt nodded towards Emily. "Couldn't have done it without you. Take care of yourself Emily."

Bennell and Emily walked back towards the state troopers as more vehicles, Army trucks, rolled up to stop behind the road block of police cars.

Wayne and Wyatt stepped out into the street. Soldiers came charging past them and on into Santa Mira. There was sporadic gunfire coming from the center of Santa Mira now.

"Who the hell are you?" A colonel came striding along and stopped to study Wayne and Wyatt.

Wyatt smiled. "Concerned citizens."

"Bullshit!" The colonel spit out. "Son, I am an excellent judge of people and I can spot trouble when I see it. I suggest you explain how it is you are here and not one of these pod things." Another officer, a lieutenant, came up next to the colonel.

"We are government agents." Wayne said carefully sliding out his ID from inside his jacket. Wyatt did the same and they handed them over to the colonel.

The colonel studied them for a moment. "This doesn't mean anything to me." He said as he handed the two IDs to the lieutenant next to him. The lieutenant glanced at them and then quickly tugged at the colonel's sleeve. He spoke quickly and quietly to the colonel. The colonel's face wrinkled as he seemed to be surprised.

"Oh, well, I guess, you are somebody after all. I am Colonel Bruckner. Uh, is there anything you need?" Bruckner asked. His voice was much calmer now.

Wayne shook his head. "I don't think so. Thank you, Colonel Bruckner."

"Hey." Wyatt got Wayne's attention. He pointed towards the east. "Isn't that towards the agricultural station?"

Wayne looked east. The sky was glowing red in that direction. "I think it is."

Bruckner followed their gaze. "Ah, that would be the 4th Platoon. They were moving in from Salt Springs."

"Well, with your permission, we'll tag along on the clean up here." Wayne said to Bruckner.

Bruckner nodded and waved towards the town. "Knock yourself out."

Wayne and Wyatt started walking into the center of Santa Mira. They could here gunshots coming from various directions. They had walked a short while without talking. They had picked up their guns and there were bodies scattered about the street.

"Well," Wyatt said, "this was different."

Wayne nodded slightly. "I have to agree. Not really what we were expecting."

To Wyatt's right there was an odd groaning sound. He turned and a pod-person was still alive. It started to crawling towards Wyatt. He turned and shot the creature in the head.

"I think that one was already dying." Wayne said.

"No sense taking any chances." Wyatt said with a shrug.

Out of the doorway of a Dry Cleaners store front to the left of Wayne an individual stumbled. It hung on the door frame for a moment staring at Wayne and Wyatt with cold empty eyes. There was a stream of greenish fluid running down the side of it. Wayne raised his arm and fired twice hitting it once in the chest and once in the throat. The pod-person slid to the sidewalk and stopped moving.

Wayne looked over at Wyatt whose gaze held a trace of a question.

Wayne shrugged. "Let's go ahead and be sure."

Wyatt nodded. "Good idea."

They walked on down the main street of Santa Mira.

K McConnell

www.kmcconnellbooks.com[1]

kmcconnell@kmcconnellbooks.com

1. http://www.kmcconnellbooks.com/

The Hamlet Mysteries series...

To Not Be In Hamlet

Sam MacNeil, part time mystery writer, has returned to his hometown to house sit for his parents as they start a lengthy vacation. What Sam has forgotten while away is the quirky weirdness of the little town of Hamlet. With expectations that he would quietly do his time in Hamlet the discovery of a dead body, clearly murdered, changes everything. Now Sam finds, much to his chagrin, the residents of Hamlet are expecting him to solve the murder. Not only does Sam not want to be involved in it, but the authroities have made it clear his help is not wanted. Was it the angry businessman from Detroit? Was it the shifty handyman the victim worked with? Sam doesn't know, but when killers from Detroit show up the situation is taking a serious and deadly turn. And then there's Becky. An old friend who clearly has more than friendship on her mind. Murder, killers and romance...this is not how this brief stay in Hamlet was supposed to go.

The Art of Hamlet

An old family friend asks Sam to look into a break in at her house. She is an art collector and critic, but nothing has been stolen and the only thing disturbed are some small statues. While it is a puzzling incident Sam doesn't think it is a serious issue, but when a neighbor is murdered and found bobbing in a nearby lake the story is once again taking a dark turn. As usual Sam is not inclined to get involved in a murder investigation, but somehow he seems to be sliding in that direction anyway. In addition, the County Detective seems to have recognized that Sam might be of some use—-regardless of the consequences for Sam. And what of Sam's old classmate, who is now a seemingly crazy hermit, ranting on about terrorists in Hamlet? Is that actually possible? To complicate things even further something is happening between Sam and Becky. Love and Death seem to be chasing Sam through the wacky streets of Hamlet.

Ophelia's Hunt

Sam's women troubles have seemingly tripled. There is Becky and the relationship that Sam has found himself in with her. However, suddenly, there is Callie. Sam's wealthy and wild ex-fiance who has appeared in Hamlet. Is she here to get Sam back? Everyone thinks so—-including Becky. Then there's the beautiful woman named Misty. She seems to have a particular interest in Sam as well. And, of course, there's murder in Hamlet once again. Questions abound. Is the lovely Misty a suspect or a new love interest? Who are the men stalking Callie? How is Sam going explain all of this to an increasingly angry Becky? Why is the County Detective actually soliciting Sam's help? Should Sam be flattered or very careful? With love and murder swirling around Sam how is he going to survive this?

The Ghosts of Hamlet

Sam MacNeil, part time writer, is house sitting for his parents in his hometown of Hamlet. The people of Hamlet are far more quirky than Sam remembers from his childhood and he is keen on leaving them behind and getting his life back, but it's those dead bodies that are the real problem. They just keep showing up. Murder in the small town of Hamlet has taken a noticeable uptick since Sam has returned and the residents have taken notice. Sam claims it has nothing to do with him and yet...Now, even worse, the residents are seeing ghosts and they blame Sam for that as well.

Sam may get his chance to escape Hamlet now that his parents are heading home, but can he really walk away without solving the mystery of the ghosts? Will he get away before the "gangsters" from Detroit catch up with him and turn him into a ghost? And what about Becky? He really wasn't planning on a romantic entanglement to muddle things up.

So what do ghosts, gangsters, girlfriends, musk ox and talking cans of beans all have in common? Sam MacNeil and the quirky town of Hamlet, of course.

The Play of Hamlet

It is finally here. The Founder's Day festival in Hamlet. A gala event highlighted by a play depicting the bizarre founding of Hamlet. Sam is not only the star of the play, but also a target for Scanlon and his killers from Detroit. They are determined to finish him off once and for all. But Sam knows they are coming and, with the help of the quirky residents of Hamlet, he has his own plans in the works. What Sam doesn't know is that Scanlon isn't the only killer from Sam's past that is out to get him. Could the biggest day of the year in Hamlet be Sam's last?

The King of Hamlet

The sixth story in the Hamlet Mystery series starts out where most of the stories end up...with a dead body. The trouble is Sam is found standing over the dead body and refusing to explain what has happened. He seems willing to take the fall for the guy's murder, but he is clearly hiding something. His friends are sure he didn't commit murder, but who is he protecting and why? What Sam is not telling anyone is that he is playing a more dangerous game than any of them can imagine. As bodies begin piling up around Sam he is increasingly wondering if he has a guardian angel or has become an unwilling accomplice to the Angel of Death. Once again women and murder are causing headaches for Sam.

The Graves of Hamlet

As if the town of Hamlet didn't have enough trouble with dead bodies now, it appears, someone is digging them up in the cemetary. The quirky residents of Hamlet are sure this has something to do with Sam. As usual Sam doesn't really want anything to do with whatever is going on, but when someone tries to make the cemetary Sam's premanent home one dark night it would seem that Sam will need to sort this out—-if only to save himself. To add to the confusion, with Becky out of town, Sam must also figure out who the half naked woman is that keeps showing up on his deck sun bathing. Oh, and who are these other guys that just showed up in Hamlet? The grandson of the recently deceased retired cop who is lying about his real identity and the suspicious looking guy casually asking questions around town about the same dead cop...?

Polonius' Plight

Here's a surprise...there's been a murder in Hamlet—-again. This time, however, Sam is very much intentionally involved. It's the suspects. The guy was found with a gaping shotgun blast to the chest. Like the one in the trunk of Renee's car. Of course the last person to be seen with the murder victim was Jen—-and she seems to have disappeared. And why is Reese, the County Detective looking for Becky and her grandfather's .38? Sam is sure none of his friends are murderers, but to keep any and all of them out of jail he needs to find out who the killer is and fast. To make matters worse, while Sam is trying to solve a murder and hide his friends the Town Council of Hamlet has had enough of Sam and the murders that seem to follow him around. They passed yet another of their many bizarre ordinances. Sam has been ordered to leave Hamlet.

The Office of Scientific Operations

With the conclusion of the traumatic events in 1933 surrounding the shocking affair involving the city of New York and a beast commonly referred to as "King Kong", the president of the United States, Franklin Roosevelt, established the Office of Scientific Operations (OSO). The purpose of the OSO was to monitor and evaluate the level of risk and assist in any manner the mitigation of danger of any and all scientific operations and anomalies. With the rapid pace of scientific discovery this office was given the highest priority and clearance to investigate any potential threats or consequences to the interests of the United States of America.

What follows are the real stories behind the cinematic cover-ups presented to the general public...

Release #1 from the declassified files of the Office of Scientific Operations...

From 1953...

File #153 (commonly referred to by the public as "The Beast from 20,000 Fathoms")

OSO agents Elliot Simms and Robbie Regan, while observing an atomic test in the Arctic, are unwittingly caught up in the release of prehistoric beasts from millions of years of suspended animation in the ice. Now they must help in stopping this new terror as it moves steadily down the east coast destroying anything in it's path.

From 1954...

File #157 (commonly referred to by the public as "Them")

OSO agents Simms and Regan investigate the odd circumstances surrounding a missing FBI agent only to stumble upon a horror in the New Mexico desert and if they cannot find a way to stop it there is a very good chance this could be the end of humanity.

Release #2
from the declassified files of the
Office of Scientific Operations...

From 1954...

File #159 (commonly referred to by the public as "Terror in the Jungle")

OSO agent Jonathon Wyatt is pulled off vacation to an island in Indonesia to investigate sightings of pteranodons. The island is not far from the island known infamously as Z Land. It was once the headquarters of Dr. Zeitner whose experiments in genetically manipulating prehistoric monsters terrorized the world in the 1930s before the OSO put a stop to it. Wyatt's job is to determine if these are indeed Dr. Zeitner's creatures, but what he finds is much more deadly. This is no way to spend a vacation—-trying not to get eaten.

Release #3
from the declassified files of the
Office of Scientific Operations...

From 1954...

File #161 (commonly referred to by the public as "Revenge of the Creature")

After the capture of an unknown species of half man half fish is brought back to a Florida marine institute, OSO agents Wayne and Wyatt must determine the risk to the American people it poses. When the creature escapes and begins terrorizing the citizens of Florida the risk becomes all too real. Now they must hunt it down and stop it's killing spree, if they can.

From 1955...

File #165 (commonly referred to by the public as "It Came From Beneath the Sea")

OSO agents Simms and Regan are sent out to Pearl Harbor to investigate damage to one of the Navy's most advanced atomic submarines by some kind of giant creature. While the Navy has a hard time believing it, the OSO knows such creatures are real. It soon becomes apparent by the large number of ships being lost that something dangerous is hunting throughout the Pacific. Now, with the creature openly attacking the west coast of the United States Simms and Regan join the fight to stop this thing before the entire Pacific is destroyed by it.

Release #4
from the declassified files of the
Office of Scientific Operations...

From 1954...

File #163 (commonly referred to by the public as "The DC Creeper")

On a break from hunting monsters for the Office of Scientific Operations, OSO Agent Wyatt is trying to adjust to a more crowded domestic life. As brutally murdered bodies begin showing up in the nation's capitol, though, this doesn't seem like it is going to be much of a break. The newspapers have dubbed the hulking killer "The Creeper" and it looks like Wyatt is going to have to hunt him down and stop him before Wyatt becomes the next victim.

Release #5
from the declassified files of the
Office of Scientific Operations...

From 1956...

File #166 (commonly referred to by the public as "Tarantula")

Agents Simms and Regan from the Office of Scientific Operations, the OSO, returning from the Pacific Coast having just finished dealing with yet another monster threatening the United States are redirected to a small town in Arizona to verify that a large tarantula that has been terrorizing the local inhabitants has been destroyed by the Air Force. With Beka, a woman who insists on tagging along with the intrepid agents—-a clear violation of official regulations—-in tow, they quickly discover that the threat of the giant spiders in the Arizona desert are not over just yet.

From 1956...

File #171 (commonly referred to by the public as "Invasion of the Body Snatchers")

The Office of Scientific Operations, the OSO, has sent agents Wayne and Wyatt out to the small California city of Santa Mira to locate a missing Air Force major, sent to investigate the impact of some meteors, and to understand the meaning of his last cryptic message to Washington. What they find is that, while the city of Santa Mira may look like a quaint place to visit it soon becomes apparent that a missing Air Force major is the least of Wayne and Wyatt's problems. There is something very strange and deadly going on in Santa Mira. Something that seems...alien?

The New Sheriff

Travis Ames, somehow, has developed super powers. Exactly what these powers entail he's not sure. He's still learning how to control his powers, but he's already decided that he should use this new found power to fight crime. And...if he made a little profit along the way, well, that wouldn't be so bad either. But reality has a way of altering the best laid plans. He has quickly figured out he has no idea how to go about crime fighting. And, to make matters worse, he has learned the hard way, his new powers won't protect him from getting hurt or, quite possibly, killed. Can he survive long enough to learn how to use his powers? Can he get an aging detective to teach him how to fight crime? Can he prevent Aubrey, the new girl, and everyone else at work from figuring out what he can do? How long can he keep this up before he makes that one small mistake and ends up dead?

Don't miss out!

Visit the website below and you can sign up to receive emails whenever K McConnell publishes a new book. There's no charge and no obligation.

https://books2read.com/r/B-A-CGLDB-FXQVC

BOOKS 2 READ

Connecting independent readers to independent writers.

Also by K McConnell

Office of Scientific Operations
Office of Scientific Operations - Release #1

The Hamlet Mysteries
The Hamlet Mysteries 1
The Hamlet Mysteries 3

Standalone
A Conspiracy in Blood
Symbiotic Puppets
The Plague
The Club of the Bombastic Few
The Master Switch
Hamlet On A Budget
The New Sheriff
Office of Scientific Operations - Declassified Files (Release #2)
Office of Scientific Operations Release #3
Office of Scientific Operations - Declassified Files (Release #4)
Office of Scientific Operations - Declassified Files (Release #5)
The Hamlet Mysteries 2

Office of Scientific Operations - Release #6
The Hamlet Mysteries 1 - 9
The Trench of the Dead
The Heart of a Monster

Watch for more at www.kmcconnellbooks.com.

www.ingramcontent.com/pod-product-compliance
Lightning Source LLC
LaVergne TN
LVHW041035150826
845672LV00001B/336